Follow

the

Palm

Cyberworld Publishing

Cyberworld Publishing

www.cyberworldpublishing.com

First published by Cyberworld Publishing in 2014
Cover design by Cyberworld Publishing © 2014
Cover photo: Background: Manipulated: Copyright: Dhoxax, Palm leaf Manipulated: Copyright: lokes, all from Depositphotos.com
E-book ISBN: 978-1-922187-94-9
Print ISBN: 978-1-922187-95-6

Cyberworld Publishing
Jindalee St
Toronto, 2283 NSW
Australia

Follow the Palm

Charlotte Diamond Mysteries Book 9

by

Olivia Stowe

Table of Contents

Chapter One: The Dastardly Deeds

Walt Miller and Clippers raised their heads at the same time. Both were perking up their ears at what normally would be the sound of silence other than the usual frog and cricket sounds at the edge of the swamp at the back of the old Thompson property on Hopewell's River Street. Against the natural noises of the night, neither really had brought the increasingly louder sound of the powerful engines of a water craft fully forward in their consciousness until the sound had suddenly stopped. This, despite how unusual it was to hear a motor craft on this section

7

of Maryland's Choptank River at this time of night in the fall and also despite Walt having expected something of this nature. The summer-only river residents had been gone for a month or more, so this should be a quiet time of the year.

Once detected, neither the sound of the motor nor that it had ceased surprised Walt all that much.

It had been near midnight when Clippers, the basset hound, had insisted on being walked—or, at least, that was the story Walt would be giving if accosted. Walking to the edge of the swamp area from the backyard of Walt's house on Spring Street, which ran into River, was a shorter distance than taking the street route. Besides, Walt was in his pajamas, robe, and slippers, not a sight he wanted to subject any late street strollers in the small town of Hopewell to, although he did it often and knew it backed up his story for being out here on the edge of the swamp at night.

Clippers had done his business, and Walt had pulled off the path into the dense underbrush to wait and observe. But the sound of silence now was pierced with the scrape of metal bumping up against tree trunks, accompanied by an expletive rendered in a low, muffled voice.

And then a sound came from another direction, from the edge of the grounds of the rest home Brenda Boynton and Charlotte Diamond had opened up for retired movie folks on a peninsula thrusting into the Choptank. Walt turned toward this new sound, and was about to utter words of recognition and query when the plank of wood hit him full in the face and he dropped to the ground like a rock.

Clippers gave a pained yelp as a well-aimed kick connected with his stomach. Walt had dropped the dog's leash when he went down, and the kick propelled Clippers off the pathway rimming the edge of the swamp. The plank of wood lashed out again into the undergrowth there, but it didn't connect with anything. Whatever direction Clippers had careened off in, he just kept on moving. Finally, he settled a bit off from the path, unwilling to leave his master, and bayed at the sky briefly—but only briefly, as the sound of feet churning through the undergrowth in his direction made him go silent and sent him lumbering off into the trees behind the Thompson lot.

Low voices, conversing and cursing, over where Walt lay, wrapped up quickly, with the only sound above the frogs and crickets now being that of something being dragged through the undergrowth, followed once again by that of waves lapping against the hull of a moving boat. Then the dominant sound became that of powerful engines revving up and slowly diminishing into the distance. This was followed by just the sounds of the frogs and crickets—and of Clippers' snuffling as he returned to follow the drag marks up toward the rest home property.

* * * *

Larry Stanton slowly shut the door to Madge Miller's room at the Curtain Call rest home and touched the arm of the nurse who was leaning against the wall next to the door and dabbing her eyes with a handkerchief.

"I suppose you will have to call Evonne Clagett and ask her to come in, Anne. And please don't talk to anyone else about this yet."

"I didn't . . . I promise I didn't . . ."

"I'm sure it will all be fine, Anne. I know you wouldn't have done that. Please, just go call Evonne. And, if you could, could you send the night orderly here to stand at the door? No one should disturb the room until the police arrive."

"Yes, Doctor," a sniffling Anne said. "I didn't, though . . . you know I wouldn't . . ."

"I'm sure it had nothing to do with you Anne," Doctor Stanton answered, laying a calming hand on her arm and then giving her a gentle push to send her down the corridor to do what he'd asked. As she walked away, he pulled out his cell phone and punched in a number, and then, when he got no response to that, he punched in another. "Deputy Burch?" he whispered into the telephone.

"Yes, doctor, what do you need?" David Burch, the Talbot County deputy sheriff responsible for the area that Hopewell, Maryland, was in, answered, having seen the doctor's name on his phone.

"I'm sorry," Stanton said, still keeping his voice low, "Sheriff Wainwright wasn't picking up his phone. We need police presence at Curtain Call as soon as possible, I think."

"I'll be right over. What's the problem?"

"There's been a death. A suspicious death, I'm afraid."

"Staff or inmate—sorry, resident?" David could kick himself. He wasn't the only one who referred to the Curtain Call residents as inmates—but only as a joke. In fact, he resented that some of the more curmudgeonly residents of the rest home acted like they were prisoners. He knew those old theater folks were living in the lap of luxury, all provided by his good friends, Brenda Boynton and Charlotte Diamond.

"Resident. A fairly new one. Madge Miller."

"I'll be right there," Burch said.

As the call clicked off, Doctor Stanton looked up to see Anne coming back down the hall.

"The orderly?" he asked.

"I couldn't find him. It should be Mrs. Clagett's nephew, Kurt, but he isn't at his station. I called Mrs. Clagett, though. She's at the farm on the other end of town. She should take just a couple of minutes to get here. I'll be happy to stand by the door . . . that is, if you trust me."

"Certainly I do," Doctor Stanton said. Regardless, however, he made no move to abandon his position beside the door himself. "I guess I should call Brenda and Charlotte too," he said, as he pulled out his cell phone again.

As he finished that conversation, Evonne Clagett, the executive director of the retirement community bounced in. The term was fitting, as she was a bubbly little redheaded bundle of bustle and capability.

"This is disturbing," she said in hushed tones as she approached. Everyone who worked at Curtain Call was accustomed to speaking in low and calm tones in the halls of the rest home, no matter how difficult the situation at hand was. When the elderly congregated, they could be set off in agitation by the mere hint of something new or out of the ordinary happening in their midst. "Madge Miller seemed quite healthy. Were there any signs of distress this evening, Anne?"

"No, ma'am, there weren't," Anne was quick to add. "Her son was visiting this evening, and she was quite animated and talkative."

"Her son? Walt Miller was here?" Walt owned the town barber shop and was married to the town clerk, Mary, who operated the village beauty shop. Madge Miller had owned a movie theater down in Richmond, Virginia, before moving into Curtain Call to be near her son. It had been somewhat of a favor to Walt and Mary that she had been accepted as a resident, because her interviews upon entering the home indicated she would be quite cantankerous, and she showed no great interest in being there. But she wasn't a scholarship resident, and she qualified for residency. She had worked with movies in Hollywood before buying the movie theater in Richmond. She was well-heeled and paid full price, which was a bit steep considering the first-class amenities provided at Curtain Call.

"No, her other son, Wendell Miller, visiting from down south," Anne said. "He said he was staying at the Vales' B&B up the street."

"I guess I'd better call him, and Walt as well," Evonne said. "But first, you look concerned, Larry. Is there a problem with the death?"

"Yes, there is, Evonne," the doctor said. "The death is suspicious. There's a syringe beside the body. And my preliminary findings are of a drug overdose." Upon saying this, the doctor, lifted a hand, encased in a surgical glove. He was holding a small plastic packet that had a symbol embossed in it in green—a stylized palm tree. "There is residue of a white powder in this and there was all of the paraphernalia needed to liquefy it on the counter in her kitchenette."

"I didn't, I swear . . . I would never . . . I found her that way," Anne wailed as Evonne reached out to her to keep her from slumping down the wall beside the closed door to Madge Miller's room.

Her wail became matched by the sound of the siren of an approaching police car and by the buzzing of the concerned voices of Brenda Boynton and Charlotte Diamond as the two women appeared at the far end of the corridor.

Chapter Two: Not So Welcome Morning's Light

"You look tired today, Charlotte. Didn't sleep well?"

"Well, everything that happened when we actually tried to go to sleep was downhill," Charlotte answered. Both women laughed, and hearing them do so was taken by Sam and Rocket as fun that was happening without them. The two dogs woke from fantasizing about the ducks swimming out by the pier and came to their mistresses, who were sitting on the bank of the river—Sam to Charlotte and Rocket to Brenda.

Charlotte continued. "I did get to sleep fine, but I heard that motorboat again out on the river. The third time recently. Wish I knew who took their motorboat out that early in the morning. We do have a town noise ordinance about that—for very good reason." Charlotte took her duties as Hopewell mayor probably more seriously than the good citizens of Hopewell thought she would when they took advantage of her missing a town meeting to vote her into office.

"I didn't hear a thing."

Charlotte almost delivered a horselaugh. Brenda had put earphones on to listen to that "wave upon wave" supposedly soothing sound, blocking most other sounds, as soon as Charlotte gave her the last kiss and rolled away from her in the bed.

"I slept the sleep of the dead," Brenda said. "I think I sleep better in your cottage than in my house. I certainly doubt I'll get good sleep at Pattie's. Suppose we could just call her and tell her there's an investigation going on here that we can't leave?"

Charlotte Diamond turned and looked at her wife, sitting in the other Adirondack chair in the backyard of Charlotte's Hopewell cottage overlooking the Choptank River. Brenda Boynton was busy making Origami swans with her hands. They were exquisite even though Brenda had just taken up the art. Brenda was immediately good at any art she took up. Charlotte, who was somewhat lumbering and uncoordinated in everything but brainpower would have been slightly disgusted with the mature movie star's artistic talents if she didn't worship Brenda.

"The way Sheriff Wainwright shuffled us out of Curtain Call last night indicates he doesn't want us anywhere close to the investigation of this—which is quite all right with me," Charlotte said.

Brenda gave her a snort of disbelief. She'd never known the former FBI agent she'd married to shy away from a mystery.

"And he's justified," Charlotte continued. "We own the place, so we shouldn't be seen to be involved in the investigation at all."

"Which doesn't mean that you'll stay out of the sleuthing, does it?" Brenda said and lit up the surrounding shaded lawn with her signature tinkling laugh and glorious smile. She wasn't criticizing Charlotte. As a retired senior FBI agent whose skills were still being sought for consultancy work by the Annapolis FBI office, Charlotte was, by far, the best person within fifty miles of Hopewell to get to the bottom of Madge Miller's questionable death.

"Damn right I'm not just going to stand back. Madge Miller's death shouldn't be too complicated to solve, if Haws Wainwright does some checking down in Richmond. I don't know how she might have gotten the heroin, but she's looked a little dopey to me since she moved into the retirement community. Chances are it was a self-inflicted overdose."

"But you don't think Haws will contact Richmond right away, do you?"

"No. The man couldn't investigate his way out of a taco shell. I'll be glad when the voters replace him with David Burch. Now that young man has promise."

"You've already made phone calls, haven't you?"

"Called Evan this morning. He promised to make some inquiries down in Richmond." Evan Worthington was a long-ago—and still would be, if he had his way—suitor of Charlotte's who also was the head of the FBI Annapolis office and Charlotte's sometime colleague now that he'd convinced her to do some consulting with the office she once had worked in.

"So you think this might be wrapped up fairly quickly, and I have no excuse to decline Pattie's offer? That's too . . . oh, all right, Rocket. I can work on these swans later. Obviously your nose needs to be in my lap at this very moment . . . and your paw too. But I draw the line at that big rump of yours." Brenda gave a tinkling laugh, and the boxer the couple had inherited, Rocket, gave a little woof as he won his battle for attention.

Their other dog—also inherited—Sam, a Siberian husky, had left Charlotte's side and was loping up toward the front of the cottage, on River Street, to meet and greet another neighborhood dog that was approaching. Although Brenda and Charlotte's permanent residence now was the federal mansion up River Street that had once been the plantation house for the whole area and was Brenda's ancestral home, the two women and their dogs—under the supervision of their housekeeper, Bea Helgerson—were living temporarily in the River Street cottage, near the retirement home end of River Street. This had been Charlotte's retirement home before Brenda returned to Hopewell from Hollywood and the two met.

Brenda had decided that, after some 120 years, it was time to do extensive renovations of her house. The timing of the decision was pushed because after the two owners of the Curtain Call retirement community had gotten married—thanks to the change in the Maryland same-sex marriage laws earlier that year—Charlotte had decided that her cottage would make an ideal reception center for Curtain Call. It was positioned just a few lots short of the gates into the retirement community and a small shopping and services center for the residents had been constructed between it and the retirement home gates. But now the conversion of the cottage would have to wait until the renovations were complete on Brenda's house.

"I know you won't back out of your commitment to the Spoleto Festival in Charleston, so we'll be there anyway," Charlotte responded. "We'll just have to get the matter of Madge Miller cleared up in the next two weeks."

The Spoleto Festival, the darling of the recently deceased composer Gian Carlo Menotti, took its name from a sister festival in Menotti's Italian home town of Spoleto. For two weeks in late May to early June every year, Charleston gave over its performance venues in and around the central city College of Charleston to a series of music, dance, and theater performances. This year, Brenda, who was as good a torch song singer as she was a top box office movie actress, had been invited to give four singing performances at the festival and to become somewhat of a celebrity centerpiece for the two-week event. She had accepted and, when she had, an actress she had worked with in movies— not particularly a friend, Brenda acknowledged, though it took quite a bit of bad relations not to count as a friend of Brenda's— had invited Brenda and Charlotte to stay with her at her tea plantation on the ocean front south of Charleston.

Charlotte had been leery about the invitation but hadn't objected. She still was a little skittish about the two women being married and also in the public eye, but Brenda had laughed and said, "That's no problem. One of the reasons I was standoffish with her when we were working in movies together is that she kept propositioning me."

After the snort, Charlotte said, "And so she's enticed you down to Charleston to have her way with you?"

"Not with the wife I have."

Both laughed. It was the closest Brenda would come to commenting on Charlotte's large-boned (and large girthed) stature in contrast to her own trim figure. Although in her late fifties, Brenda was still a beauty who caused the public to sigh and tune in to her melodious voice and distinctive laugh and smile whenever she was on the screen. Charlotte, pushing sixty

19

hard, wasn't exactly plain herself, but she certainly was zaftig and cut a commanding figure, which had stood her in good stead as an FBI agent.

Charlotte was still thinking of a rejoinder to that remark when their attention was arrested by barking from the street. Rocket lifted his head out of Brenda's lap, with his ears standing straight up, and bounded out toward the River Street curb, where Sam was planted in Charlotte's front yard and barking at the third dog that had appeared and was equally planted on River Street and barking back.

The women knew the dog and knew that Clippers was friendly with their own two dogs, so something else clearly was wrong.

The two women pulled themselves out of their chairs and turned toward the street.

"It's the Millers' dog, Clippers," Brenda said. "He's dragging his leash. I wonder—"

But she wasn't able to state what she wondered about, because Charlotte's cell phone was ringing. She was looking a bit ashen and very much concerned when she flipped the phone closed. "That was David Burch," she said in a hushed voice. "He's asking me to come over to the back lawn of Curtain Call, down near the woods separating the lawn from the swamp. Walt Miller's body has been found in the grass there. His head's been bashed in."

"Oh, dear. That's what Clippers . . . he wanted us to follow him to Walt. Walt. Oh no, Madge Miller and now her son."

"Yes, her death may not have had as simple an explanation as I thought it would be," Charlotte said, as the two women set out to follow Clippers' lead back to Walt's body.

* * * *

Once he'd gotten the women and Sam and Rocket to follow him, Clippers had run ahead, beyond their reach. When he got to the group surrounding his master, he went down on his belly near the body, his job done after several hours of trying to get someone's attention, and let out an exhausted sigh.

The bundle of clothing Sheriff Wainwright and Deputy Burch were standing around, with the county medical examiner, Sharon Como, bent over the body, was barely on Curtain Call property. Brenda and Charlotte approached from around the corner of the complex, Charlotte striding purposefully toward the group of officials and Brenda hanging back a bit with Sam and Rocket protectively at her sides. The torso of the body was on the grassy verge of the lawn and the legs were in the undergrowth that marked the start of the parkland going down to the edge of the swamp. A few other policemen were roaming around the area, looking for clues, and David Burch went off to talk to one who had emerged from the tree line toward the swamp as the women walked up.

Brenda only took one look at the crime scene and then muttered that she'd take Rocket and Sam home for Bea to look after and would return after that.

Sheriff Wainwright didn't look any too happy to see Charlotte, who had bested him continually on cases and had put him on the edge of being tossed out of office because of questions of corruption. But the body had been found on the edge of the retirement community property and Charlotte, along with Brenda, owned the retirement community. He'd have to include them in this to some extent whether he liked it or not.

"Wonder what he was doing out here in his pajamas and robe," Wainwright said when Charlotte and Brenda reached where Walt still lay.

"Walking Clippers, no doubt," Charlotte answered. Was the sheriff that much of an idiot, she wondered. Did he think the residents of Hopewell ran around town in their pajamas at night just for the hell of it? Walt walked his dog on the park trail by the swamp many nights. The old dog was getting too old to hold it all night. Walt probably thought no one knew he didn't bother to dress to take Clippers out at night, but of course everyone in town knew about his nocturnal dog walks.

"Clippers?"

"The dog. The basset hound here. This is Walt's dog. The poor guy has probably been running around trying to get

22

someone's attention ever since this happened. How long has Walt been out here? You have any guess on time of death?" Charlotte was addressing the medical examiner directly, ignoring the sheriff. The relations between the two women were a bit touchy, but that was mostly one sided. Sharon Como had it in her mind that Charlotte, who came from full access to the resources of the FBI's labs, looked down on a mere county medical examiner. But in that she was wrong; Charlotte respected Sharon's abilities. Her formal approach to Como was more one of respecting her authority than second-guessing her.

"Cause of death was blunt force trauma to the head," Como said, not looking up, as if not looking up would leave the impression that she was responding to the sheriff. She didn't have much more respect for Haws Wainwright than Charlotte did. "Something woody, I'd say. There are wood splinters in the wound. Dead maybe seven or eight hours given the weather conditions and the state of rigor. Not much blood here, though, and there should be plenty, if this is the where the attack occurred."

The three who were standing involuntarily looked around. "The drag marks look like they come from the direction of the swamp rather than the Curtain Call buildings," Charlotte said.

"Thank god for that," muttered Brenda, who had returned from taking the dogs back to the cottage. Then, embarrassed that her first thought was for the retirement home, she added, "Has anyone called Mary yet?"

"I did, yes," David Burch said, as he rejoined the group. He had disappeared for a few minutes, having accompanied the policeman who had been talking with him into the wooded area toward the swamp. "She thought he was still in bed. He sleeps late. And they sleep in separate rooms because . . . Mrs. Miller says it's because she snores."

No one laughed, although it was evident that the sheriff was having trouble holding it in.

"Think you need to come look at what Nate found, Sheriff," Burch said. "Maybe you too, Ms. Diamond."

The sheriff reddened up, but he resisted saying anything. He didn't appreciate at all the good working relations between his deputy and the retired FBI agent, but there was little he could do about it. He realized that Deputy Burch was far more popular with the voters of the county then he was—and Charlotte Diamond was the mayor of this little burg. And he had his own reelection as sheriff coming up in the near future.

"I'll go up to Curtain Call," Brenda said. "Someone should be with Mary at this time. I'll send Evonne over there. They are good friends. And I'll hold down the fort for Evonne while she's gone. Maybe I'd better call Chuck Dawson too." Dawson was the retirement community's lawyer—as well as Brenda's and Charlotte's.

"And I'll take Clippers' too, if he'll come with me," Brenda added. "Evonne can take him back to Mary. he's done his duty."

Charlotte and Sheriff Wainwright followed David Burch and the young policeman, Nate, through the woods to the edge of the swamp. It wasn't lost on any of them that they were following drag marks, with smears of blood on the smashed-down ferns.

"This looks like where Miller was assaulted, Sheriff," Burch said as they came to the pathway following the edge of the swamp. "And come over here, at the edge of the swamp. The mud shows there's been a boat pulled up to the bank here."

"I heard the motors of a boat out on the river about the time Sharon said Walt was killed," Charlotte said.

"I'd heard there had been motorboat activity on the river late at night," the deputy said. "We've had some complaints, and it's been on my to-do list to put a police boat out in the water to see if we could stop that. It looks like the boat came into land here while Walt was walking his dog and there was a fight of some sort. Wonder what would cause that, though?"

"That's two Millers in one night," Sheriff Wainwright said. "That's one too many Millers to die for this whole shit not to be suspicious."

For the first time in some time Charlotte had to admit that Sheriff Wainwright had latched on to the most important issue running. If there was one thing she didn't put much stock in, it was coincidences.

"Evonne told me that Walt's brother was here visiting the mother," Charlotte said. "I understand he's staying at the Vales' B&B across the street from Brenda's house. Has someone—?"

"He's not there anymore," Wainwright said. "We've been here since we were called in on the mother's death. We were told that the son—the other son, not Walt—was the last one to see the old woman. That he'd visited her last night. And the nurse said they'd had some loud words, although she hadn't heard a peep out the Miller woman after the son left. So we called over to the Vales'. Todd went looking for the guy— Wendell Miller—but his room was empty and hadn't been slept in. The guy's split."

"Do you know where he's headed or where he lives?" Charlotte asked.

"No idea," Wainwright answered. "But Todd Vale is going through the B&B records to come up with a contact number and address. Haven't heard from him yet."

"We should have the records up at Curtain Call, too," Charlotte said. "He'll be listed as a relative and would have had to check in with an address and contact number to be able to visit his mother."

"Let's go on up there then," the sheriff said. "I'm real interested in what he and his mother were having words about

26

and why he paid for a room at the B&B tonight but didn't use it. And I'm just as interested in how well he got along with his brother, Walt."

* * * *

Another one of the young policemen met them at the door of Curtain Call—they entered from the terrace into the dayroom rather than through the front entrance on the other side of the complex. The residents were out in full force, most of them gathered around circular tables in their own small cliques. Brenda and Charlotte had wondered why Evonne had insisted that the room's furnishings be set up in small conversation groups, but they had quickly learned why; the elderly could be as cliquish as teenagers could be. Brenda was going from table to table doing what calming she could do. Charlotte noticed that Brenda hadn't had much luck with the group they considered to be the troublemakers, or the "Terribles," as they called them, a group Madge Miller had settled into as soon as she'd arrived at Curtain Call.

Madge's arrival and attachment to this group had actually been a pleasant surprise to the community's staff. Movie people could be real pills, and old movie people could be especially so. This group, in particular, had been beyond difficult—homicidal even. It hadn't been long since one of the group, Gladys Morrison, a former wardrobe assistant, had been strangled by another in the group, Phil Taylor, a former movie cameraman. Stan Plaugher, a former movie stage grip had been the sole survivor of the original group of recalcitrants, whose numbers had quickly been filled in with other perpetually disgruntled, albeit pampered, members. When Madge Miller had joined them, though, the group had settled down and become almost friendly—rather lethargic, actually.

But today the four of them left in the group were being extra belligerent. Brenda was cajoling them along, with the thought that they were mostly upset that one of their number had just died an unnatural death. Natural deaths were taken in stride in this end-of-the-road home, no matter how comfortable that end of life was being made. In fact, foreseen deaths here were responded to by most of the other residents as a satisfaction that I hadn't been them—yet. But an unnatural death at this age was . . . well, unnatural. And considering they were close to death anyway, being murdered seemed almost obscene, certainly rude.

"Think you need to come to the woman's room, Sheriff, and see what we found," the young policeman said as Wainwright, Burch, and Charlotte Diamond entered the dayroom.

"What is it?" the sheriff asked.

"Think you need to see it to believe it." Wainwright, Burch, and Charlotte all followed him out of the dayroom.

"The old dame has a regular pharmacy in here," another policeman said as they entered Madge Miller's room. Madge's body had already been taken away, but the room otherwise was the way they'd found it, although it had been searched by the police. It had been gone over thoroughly enough that they had found a false back in one of the lower cupboards of the kitchenette wall, where a policeman was kneeling and pulling plastic bag after plastic bag of white powder and marihuana out of the hidden recess.

Both the sheriff and the deputy went down on their haunches to look at the stash, which kept coming out and being piled on the floor. Everything was in small packets, each with an abstract palm tree embossed on it in green.

"It's all here. Weed, cocaine, and heroin. She could serve anyone's addiction for months," one of the policemen said.

"She, or maybe someone who was using her for camouflage," Charlotte chimed in. "I don't think Madge Miller was capable of constructing that false wall without the staff noticing. And she certainly wasn't trucking those drugs in here on her walker. There's more to this than meets the eye, guys."

At that moment Brenda appeared in the doorway with a cell phone in her hand. Her eyes picked out the sheriff. "I have Todd Vale on the phone, Sheriff. He says that Wendell Miller has reappeared at the B&B and gone straight to his room. Todd hasn't told him anything about what has happened and Mr. Miller didn't ask anything about it. Todd wants to know what to do. Whether you want to come to the B&B or Mr. Miller should be asked to come here."

In an atypical smart move by the sheriff, Charlotte heard Wainwright answer, "By all means, I'll go there. And tell Mr. Vale not to say anything to Miller, please."

Chapter Three: Assessing the Damage and Liabilities

Charlotte walked back into the Curtain Call dayroom with Brenda. She was feeling sorry and apprehensive for her partner. Nearly all of Brenda's energy over the past year had gone into establishing this dream—a place where the elderly who had worked in Hollywood on movies, as Brenda had, and no matter how humble their movie work was, could come. Where they could be with folks like themselves in a comfortable environment whether or not they could afford to end their lives in such security and comfort. The comfort part had worked out fine. Brenda was wealthy, not only from family money but also from nearly forty years as a top box office draw in movies. She also had won the Maryland lottery. Most of her money had gone into her dream for Curtain Call, though, which she'd established on a peninsula at the foot of the same street as the ancestral home she'd returned to in the small Maryland village of Hopewell on the Choptank.

Brenda had come back to Hopewell as much to hide— from the death of a lover who she was being suspected of murdering—as to retire. She was still appearing in films, but mostly in cameo roles now, while helping to promote the film career of her natural-born son, Tony Trice. Other than Tony and Curtain Call, Brenda's primary emphasis in life was her new marriage to Charlotte Diamond. Charlotte had retired from the FBI and moved to a cottage in Hopewell before Brenda had returned from Hollywood. When they met, they quickly fell for each other—Charlotte never having been involved with a woman before, whereas Brenda had been. Charlotte's investigation and clearing Brenda of suspicion of murder brought the two even closer.

Charlotte bought into Brenda's Curtain Call dream to the extent of investing effort and money in it as well. She had been gratified that Brenda's dream of establishing a comfortable last stop for those who had devoted their lives to movie work was working out in terms of comfort. She was almost as distressed as she knew Brenda was, though—although Brenda, the consummate actress, wouldn't show that to anyone but someone who knew her as intimately as Charlotte did—that the concept had not proven to be as secure as they both had hoped. There had been a murder of a resident, by another resident, here within the last year. And now there was another suspicious death, not to mention the murder of a prominent town resident on the edge of the property.

Charlotte could feel Brenda slightly trembling as they walked side by side toward the main entrance to the dayroom, where Evonne, the community executive director, now stood, talking briefly to Sheriff Wainwright and Deputy Burch. The two law-enforcement officers were on their way to the Vales' B&B up the street to apprehend the surviving Miller brother and, presumably, to bring him back here to question him on his mother's death the previous evening.

Charlotte put her arm around Brenda and pulled her in close, which seemed to have a calming effect on the actress. She tensed again, though, as they were passing the table where "The Terribles" group was sitting. A former minor actor in Westerns, Blake Zane, grabbed her wrist and muttered, in an angry voice, "So, with Madge dead, where we gonna get our smack?"

The clouds rolled away from Charlotte's mind on a couple of issues and, murmuring to Brenda to continue on to Evonne, she plopped down in the empty chair next to Blake. "Are you telling me that Madge Miller was supplying you residents with drugs?"

"Sure, honey," Blake answered. The resident on the other side of him, Stan Plaugher, was trying to shush Blake. But he was unsuccessful in this. Blake was both outspoken and not the sharpest knife in the drawer. "Why'd you think the inmates in this cesspool have been so happy since Madge arrived? She kept us happy, just like old times in Hollywood. So, who supplies us now?"

"Don't you worry none about that, Blake, honey," another one of "The Terribles," Ethel Kearny, who had been a makeup artist in the same movie studio Brenda worked in, piped up. "There are more helpers around here than just Madge, and Madge done told me she was gettin' outta the business anyway. Found religion, Madge had. Seems a mite late for Madge to be doin' that, if you ask me, but I guess not if it's Catholic." The little old lady cackled at her own joke and returned to making her knitting needles go clickety-click.

Of course, Charlotte thought, as she rose from the table to leave Stan to try to explain to Blake were he'd veered off the tracks. She didn't have the time of day for Blake. He'd practically been living on the street when Curtain Call had taken him in on a no-pay residency basis. But what he said certainly did explain why "The Terribles" had been behaving so well recently. They were mellow on drugs. Having been in the movie industry, the drug culture probably wasn't a stranger to any of them. And what Blake had to say about the supplier of his drugs also pinned down whose drugs those were in the hidden compartment in Madge Miller's kitchenette cupboard.

She left the table and went over to the side of the room. Brenda and Evonne were still talking. Evonne was animated. She was a naturally animated woman—a redheaded bundle of energy—but today she looked concerned. She usually was calm, despite her vivacious expressiveness, when everyone else was running around in consternation. Of course she had every reason to be upset. A woman in her charge had died and she'd just been consoling the wife of a man found dead on the lawn of the facility she managed.

Charlotte pulled out her cell phone and punched in a familiar number. "Evan, it's me, Charlotte. I don't mean to push you, but did you find out anything about Madge Miller's background in Richmond."

"Sure did," Evan Worthington, the chief of the Annapolis FBI office that Charlotte had asked this favor from, answered. He then told her what he'd found out from the chief of the Richmond FBI office. "Had you on the list to call. Cary knew immediately who I was asking about—he asked that his regards be sent on to you, by the way."

"He knew about Madge Miller without checking?"

"Yes, seems she was quite a girl there in Richmond. She owned a theater. Bought it over a year ago, but almost immediately popped up on the police department's radar. She was up to her neck in drug distribution there, and the theater has been a major distribution point since she bought it. They never could catch her at it, but they knew it was her. They thought initially that it must be someone working for her at the theater. She was just a little old lady to them. The drug trafficking problem in the Richmond area has decreased by half since she left, though, so they decided she was the one running the operation. You say she died of a drug overdose?"

"Yes, and we've found a big enough stash of drugs in her room to indicate she was distributing here too. Evan. Thanks for the information. Would you like me to send you some of the product we found here so you can send it down to Richmond to see if it's part of the distribution system there too?"

"Sure would. You're in a very remote area, though. Wonder how it was moving and whether she was the end of that distribution line."

"I have my theory about how she's been getting it, and I'll work on whether this was the end of the line. She certainly was keeping some of the residents of Curtain Call happy."

"That settled, how about lunch sometime this week. If you didn't want to come into Annapolis, we could go halfsies and meet in Easton."

"Uh, Evan."

"I don't mean Dutch treat; I mean we can split the difference on the distance. I'm inviting both of you—my treat. I know you're happily married to Brenda now. I won't fight that. I

36

can see that it's solid between you. The invitation is for both of you."

"I'll see where we stand in a day or too, Evan. We need to get this wrapped up down here. Curtain Call is everything to Brenda and these incidents are tearing her apart—she's hiding it, but I can see it—and there's been another death here. Also, we're supposed to be off to Charleston in a bit more than a week. At least I hope we are. Brenda isn't wild about staying with this former actress she knows, but Brenda also needs a vacation from here."

"As do you, I'll bet," Evan said. "It's an open-ended invitation. Just let me know if the two of you can get away."

"Thanks, Evan. And thanks for the quick information on Madge Miller's background. That should help a lot in putting the retirement community beyond blame. Still, there must be someone else here who was helping her. And the death still looks suspicious."

Ringing off, Charlotte went over to Brenda and Evonne. "You look distressed, Evonne," she said. "You know none of this is your fault."

"That's what I've been trying to tell her," Brenda said, "But—"

"But it may be my fault," Evonne said.

"Did Mary take the news on Walt hard?"

"It's hard to say. Pastor Dunkel is with her now. But it doesn't seem to have sunk in with her. About the only thing she said while I was there was that she'd have to contact one of the other barbers to open the shop this morning. I told her no one in Hopewell would be wanting a haircut today."

"But why do you feel responsible for anything?" Charlotte asked.

"I hired them. And I should have known about Kurt."

Charlotte's face showed that she was confused.

"She's speaking of Nurse Anne and the orderly, Kurt—her husband's nephew, Kurt Clagett."

"I still don't fully understand," Charlotte said.

"I've been trying to get hold of both of them since this morning," Evonne explained. "Anne was the duty nurse and Kurt was the duty orderly last night. But neither are responding. After I left Mary's, I went on down the street to the Curtain Call staff apartments. Anne didn't answer her door. The super let me in, but Anne's not there, although there's no indication she's packed out and left. We don't know where she's gone. The Curtain Call staffers are supposed to tell us when they're out of town and leave contact numbers in case we need them in an emergency."

"And Kurt?"

"Kurt's had some run-ins with the law on drug use and distribution, but he went into rehab and was cleared by the courts. He had the credentials to be an orderly—he's working on a medical degree—and he needed the job. No one else would hire him, so I did. So, it's my fault. I hired them both and now they're gone. If they had anything to do with Madge Miller's death or the drugs stashed in her room . . . and who knows how many others . . ."

"Chances are very good that Madge Miller had the drugs herself and was distributing them," Charlotte said, choosing not to note that she probably would have needed an accomplice to get that done. Madge hadn't been all that mobile. "And we shouldn't jump to any conclusions on the rest of it for now. It certainly isn't your fault for hiring anyone. Does Kurt live with you at the farm or in one of the staff apartments?"

"No. He's still studying at Johns Hopkins in Baltimore. He lives there in a medical student dorm."

"So, he may just be in class and doesn't have his cell phone on, then," Charlotte said. "We'll contact him eventually."

"But he was supposed to be on duty last night. Doctor Stanton said that when he sent Anne to fetch him to stand by Madge's door after she died, he wasn't anywhere around. If he wasn't involved, why wasn't he where he was supposed to be?"

"There's probably a logical explanation for that. Go get yourself a cup of tea and then come back and do what you do so well—keeping the residents calm. They all are jittery about what's happening and have every right to be."

As Charlotte and Brenda watched Evonne square her shoulders and head for the staff break room, Charlotte tried to suppress the thoughts that there probably was something to Evonne's concern. Not that she was responsible for anything,

39

but that either Kurt or Anne was likely an accomplice to Madge's business. There might have been a falling out that led to Madge being killed with her own drugs, but maybe not. Maybe it was just an accident—and there was some chance that she didn't even know about the drug stash in her kitchenette and had caught someone in there and suffered the consequences.

There was no indication yet that a problem with the distribution operation had cropped up and caused anyone to panic. But, then, maybe there was if Walt's murder had something to do with mucking up the operation. And there was the possibility that the drug operation had nothing to do with Madge's death. There was that argument with her other son, Wendell. And Wendell had absconded too—although he'd come back.

Charlotte suddenly had the burning desire to know just how much Madge had been worth. Walt was dead too. If this second son needed money and Madge wouldn't give him any, just maybe . . . and maybe Wendell didn't want to share an inheritance with his brother either.

Speaking of Wendell Miller, though, Sheriff Wainwright and Deputy Burch were just then entering the main entrance of Curtain Call with a man walking between them who was looking very unhappy. Chances were excellent that this was Wendell Miller. Strangely, though, he was looking more guarded for his own welfare than in grief on having lost two family members.

Intercepting them in the foyer, however, was another policemen. He was carrying a couple of those plastic packets with a green palm tree on them in a gloved hand.

"Thought you should see these, Sheriff," he said. "We found these packets out by the murder scene at the edge of the swamp."

"The murder scene?" Wendell Miller said, in a panic. "I thought my mother died in her room and that she overdosed."

"We'll talk about that in a few minutes, Mr. Miller," the sheriff said. Then he turned to Charlotte and said, "Is there a room we can use here? And I guess there's no telling you that you can't sit in on our little chat."

"Yes and no," Charlotte said. "I'll find us a conference room." Turning to Brenda, she said, "You either go home and rest or you could help Evonne get this crowd settled down. I'll talk with you later."

As she led the sheriff and his charge off to a small conference room, what was racing through Charlotte's mind were those drug packets the young policeman had just shown the sheriff. There was little question now how the drugs were getting to Curtain Call. But there was still a question of who, beyond Madge Miller, was involved in that operation. Madge was on a walker and there was no way she had been faking how weak she was. She wasn't the one meeting a motorboat at the edge of the swamp to take possession of a periodic drugs shipment.

When she'd gotten the men settled in the conference room, Charlotte excused herself for a moment and went back out into the corridor. She reached for her cell phone again and punched in the number.

"Hi, it's me again, Evan," she spoke into the phone.

"Is it my irresistible charm?"

"Excuse me?" she said. This wasn't the day for her to focus on any sharp repartee.

"You called me just a few minutes ago. You can't get enough of me, can you?"

"Yes, Evan, it's your irresistible charm. And it's also another favor I need from you, although this one might turn out to be more of a favor for you than for me."

Chapter Four: Next to Last Stop

When Charlotte entered the conference room, she could see that the sheriff had told Wendell Miller for the first time that his brother as well as his mother was dead. It took several minutes for him to compose himself. He didn't cry, but he was taking big gulps of air to prevent doing so. When he had gotten control of himself, he managed to talk, and to be lucid when he did so, although his voice was shaky.

He seemed very convincing, Charlotte thought. But then she wondered if his reaction was a bit over the top and contrived; it struck her mind as a flag of falseness. After years and years of such questioning, she instinctively knew—most of the time—whether immediate grief was genuine or not. What Miller answered to one of the first questions the sheriff asked of him assuaged the uncertainty at the back of her mind on this point. He wasn't evasive about an issue that could bring suspicion his way.

"No, we didn't get along all that well, Walt and me," Wendell had answered. "It's more like we just didn't cross paths that often. We were split up when my parents divorced, so all we had was an early childhood together. Same city but only sporadic contact. We hadn't been friends when we were growing up. We were very different."

"Very different in what way?" Sheriff Wainwright asked.

"I'm somewhat of a wheeler and dealer, you could say. I liked the bright lights. I went with my dad, who was always playing the angles. And Walt . . . well, here he was running a barber shop in a small town."

"And what do you do for a living, Mr. Miller?"

"I own a charter plane service."

"Why did you come to Hopewell, Mr. Miller? I know it was to see your mother, but the rest home staff was surprised you even existed. All of their dealings beyond your mother were with Walt, and I think this is the first time you've visited. Where did you come from?"

"I live down in the Florida Keys. That's where the charter plane service is. Quite a bit of business down there. And I came up here because Walt called and asked me to come.

Because he couldn't get Mom to stop. That's one reason why he worked on her to leave Richmond and come live closer to him. He wanted her to stop while she still could."

"Stop distributing illegal drugs?" Wainwright asked.

Wendell paused before answering. "I guess there's nothing that could be done to her now. Yes, Mom had been a drug dealer in Richmond—on top of her legitimate business. And Walt was afraid she was doing that here too. Just from some comments the rest home residents were making when he cut the men's hair and his wife fixed the women's hair."

"And that's what you were arguing with your mother about last night?"

"Yes. She said she had no intention of stopping. Didn't even deny she was doing it. I got angry and we yelled and I stomped out and got on the road back to Florida."

"But you came back today."

"Yes, I came back. I cooled down. I decided to have another go at her. I'd come too far not to give it a good try."

"And you were the last to be with her . . . other than whoever gave her that overdose, if it wasn't self-administered."

"I don't really like what you are implying, Sheriff," Wendell said, puffing up a bit. "She was my mother. If I wanted her dead, I'd just have let her kill herself with drugs."

"The medical examiner said there was no evidence your mother was a user, Mr. Wendell. But there was evidence she had been rendered unconscious before she was injected with the heroin."

Wendell Miller took on a shocked look at that information, and Charlotte sat up straighter too. This was the first time she'd heard that. She could have kicked herself for not quizzing Sharon Como more closely. There was clearly important information the medical examiner hadn't given Charlotte—but of course there was no reason why she should have told Charlotte anything.

"I understand that your mother was quite wealthy," Wainwright continued.

"As am I, Sheriff. I'm a millionaire. Charter flying in Florida is big business. Walt was very wealthy too. I was always surprised how much he and his wife were able to put away from a barber shop and beauty salon in a hick town like this. And I'm sure when you look deeper into my mother's finances, you'll see that she cut both Walt and me out of her will. She said we already had enough, and she wasn't any more fond of us than we were of each other. If you look into her will, from what she told me, she liked this rest home so much that she was leaving all of her money to Curtain Call."

This revelation set both the sheriff and Charlotte back on their haunches, and Charlotte excused herself soon thereafter to go give Brenda the news. In one sense it was good news—in a far more unfavorable sense, though, it was a major headache. It tossed the protection and care of Madge Miller right back in Curtain Call's lap. And Curtain Call was Brenda Boynton.

When she got back to Brenda, Evonne Clagett was standing next to her and was talking on a cell phone.

"It's Nurse Anne," Brenda explained. "She was so upset last night and was hyperventilating, so she went directly to the hospital and they admitted her for the night. She hasn't abandoned her post, she was just deeply affected by Madge's death." And then when Brenda saw that Charlotte still looked concerned, she asked her what the matter was.

"I've got good news and bad news, Brenda," Charlotte answered.

When Evonne got off the phone, Brenda told her what Charlotte had found out about Madge Miller's will.

"She had told me that several times, but I just assumed she was saying it to get us all to treat her like a princess . . . not that we didn't always treat her like a princess. Her sour attitude belied any great satisfaction with Curtain Call. And . . ." Evonne paused before continuing. "Oh . . . I can see why that doesn't look good for us. And I still haven't heard from my nephew, Kurt, who was supposed to be here last night."

* * * *

Charlotte was on the phone to Evan at the FBI office in Annapolis. She, Brenda, and Evonne were sitting at the table in the staff conference room. The evening shift had come on and there were administrators enough on duty to relieve Evonne and Brenda of those responsibilities. Charlotte thought that hadn't come soon enough. Both women looked frazzled.

Charlotte was more worried, at least before she took the phone call, about Brenda than about Evonne. The executive director was diminutive in size, but she was a tower of strength and serenity—well, normally. The uncertainty of her nephew's involvement in any of this, though—a young man she'd hired himself, a relative through her husband—was wearing at Evonne in ways she'd never been challenged by before.

Brenda was another matter. She was the type of person to suffer in silence until the drop of the last straw took them to their knees without anyone expecting it. On top of that, she was the consummate actress. Only Charlotte—who was so intimate with her that they shared a bed and all that implied—knew how devoted Brenda was to Curtain Call and how much of a toll had already been taken on her to get it up and running. Charlotte was feeling very protective of her partner. She needed to get Brenda back home and occupied with other thoughts as soon as she could.

Charlotte had already called their lawyer, Chuck Dawson, in to work on the angle of Madge Miller's will and to assess the rest home's position on that—and to intervene in any press questions along those lines. The village doctor, Larry Stanton, had come in on his own. And other off-duty staffers, upon

48

hearing about the situation at Curtain Call, had come in to help. Even Nurse Anne had worked through her jitters and had shown up for her shift. Such was their regard and love for Brenda and her magnetism that they were all showing up. This was great, Charlotte knew, but she also knew it would be little comfort to Brenda—that it would be a burden to her that her friends had to do this. Charlotte wasn't sure that Brenda had the strength to bear this.

She needed to get Brenda home. Evonne needed to go home too. If Evonne cracked in public, and was seen to have done so, the woman would never be the same again. She would never be able to function as the unflappable executive director.

The phone call Charlotte was now taking would make it all worse. Evonne was watching her from across the break room table with a look on her face that revealed she knew the news was bad.

"You were right, Charlotte," Evan said. "The drug packets with the green palm trees on them have popped up in the Baltimore illegal drug stream. A lot of them at Johns Hopkins University. The lead you gave me on Kurt Clagett paid out. His photo has been IDed several times by the Baltimore police. He's distributing there."

"So, Curtain Call was just the next to last stop on this distribution thread. Thanks, Evan."

"No, thank you, Charlotte—straight from the Baltimore police. They say they owe you a big one. They haven't

49

apprehended Clagett, but now they know who to look for and how the drugs are getting into the city. They even know where the drugs are coming from. What they've analyzed have the same properties as other shipments up and down the East Coast that they've traced back to Colombia. The route comes up from South America. It's only a matter of time until they get Clagett—and, they hope, alive so that they can trace this operation up stream."

"I almost wished they didn't owe me one on this," Charlotte said.

"Well, the detective in charge of narcotics there, Jason Barnes, wanted me to give you his telephone number and said for you to call him for any help you needed. Can I give you his number?"

"Sure," Charlotte said, taking it down, although she couldn't see why she'd have need for assistance from the Baltimore police—at least assistance she would be so bold as to ask for.

After she put the number into her cell phone, Evan changed topics. "Any closer to being able to name a luncheon day?"

"If anything, a bit farther away. But maybe we'll take you up on it anyway. We both need to get away."

"Probably Brenda more than you," Evan said.

"Thanks for understanding that," Charlotte said, as her eyes met Brenda's. Brenda had never looked more bleak to

50

Charlotte—even though Charlotte had seen some of Brenda's movie where she was in far greater personal peril than this. But those were the movies, not real life.

After she delivered the bad news, she could see that Evonne was teetering on the edge. "Go home, Evonne. We can get Danny to drive you home. You don't need the staff to see how this is affecting you. They would all understand, but I know you wouldn't want that."

"Yes, perhaps that's best," Evonne answered. "I'll be back in the morning, though, happy face on and all."

"I know you will."

"But you don't have to," Brenda added. "Take all the time you need."

With Evonne gone, Charlotte turned to Brenda. "Now you, Missy."

But before she could say anything further, Dave Burch was stopping in to drop another bombshell. Sheriff Wainwright was walking Wendell Miller to a police car to take him back to the Vales' B&B.

"You missed something important, Ms. Diamond," Burch said. "The sheriff didn't tell me I could tell you, but he didn't tell me I couldn't either."

"Which is?"

"Walt Miller's death might not have been random—just being in the wrong place at the wrong time. Wendell Miller said that when Walt called him and asked him to come down and talk with their mother, Walt had already been snooping. He'd told his brother that he suspected their mother was still dealing and that her supply was coming in at night by motorboat. He wasn't walking the edge of the swamp at night just because his dog had to pee. He was snooping around to find out how the drugs were coming in."

"And maybe he did find out," Charlotte said. She was looking at Brenda, who looked like she was about to collapse.

"Yep," Burch said. "The sheriff told Miller he might have to stay around for a few days, but Miller said he had to anyway—for the funeral arrangements for both his mother and brother."

"Thanks, David. I think Brenda and I need to go back to the cottage now. Could you clear us through the police lines and any press out at the gates?"

"Sure thing, Ms. D, I'd be happy to."

Brenda gave Charlotte no opposition to leaving Curtain Call at that point—if only to go to the cottage just a couple of lots down from the front gates. That as much as anything told Charlotte that Brenda's porcelain doll aspect was coming to the front—that she was about to break.

* * * *

Charlotte learned something about Brenda that night, though, that she hadn't learned yet and that she needed to know.

Brenda wasn't a porcelain doll. She'd maneuvered through the snake pit that was Hollywood movies for nearly forty years, and she was just as strong as Charlotte was. Once having learned this, Charlotte loved her partner all the more.

They spent a quiet evening at home, with their housekeeper, Bea Helgerson, fussing around in the kitchen. Sam and Rocket—augmented by Clippers, who the women were keeping for a few days so Mary Miller didn't have to contend with a dog—sat at their feet in front of the fireplace, content that their mistresses were home. Brenda was being unusually silent and wistful, sighing now and again, and Charlotte was giving her all the space she needed to recenter herself after the rigors of the previous night and day.

"About Charleston . . ." Brenda started to say, after a lengthy silence.

"I definitely think we should go ahead and go," Charlotte said. "I think you need to get away from all of this for a bit. If you don't want to stay at that actress' home, that's fine. We can get a hotel in town. You're performing. I'm sure the Spoleto people will find a good hotel room for us."

"But you . . . there's still a mystery here. I'm sure you don't want—"

"What I want—what needs to happen," Charlotte said in what she hoped was a gentle voice—she had a bit of trouble with not being gruff and straightforward when that wasn't the best approach at that moment—"is for the two of us to be together. You should go to Charleston, and so there's no question where I will be going."

"Thank you, Charlotte," Brenda said in a small voice and sank deeper into the sofa and closer to Charlotte.

That was the last that either one of them had to say before they went to bed earlier. And if Charlotte hadn't known already how exhausted and preoccupied Brenda was, she would have known it when Brenda atypically just rolled onto her side when they got into bed and went off to sleep.

Despite this, they were both immediately fully awake at the sound of the crash down by the riverside behind the cottage. Both of them had been between sleep and wakefulness for some time before that because of the sound of the motorboat engines on the river—and more than one motorboat, it seemed to them. Brenda was the first one to pop out of the bed and head for the bedroom door. The clatter of the three dogs that had been sleeping just beyond the closed bedroom door added to the sound of Brenda's slippers as she tramped down the stairs to the first floor.

When Charlotte arrived on the back lawn, the service gun she kept in her nightstand drawer drawn, she realized both that she wasn't really needed and that Brenda had nerves and resolve of steel in contrast to the vibes she'd been sending off. One glance at the river told Charlotte that a cigarette motorboat had crashed into the cottage's pier and that two police boats were nudging into the bank. The second glance, toward where the police boat search lights were trained, revealed Brenda, looking quite fetching in her nightgown, pointing a shotgun at a young man dressed all in black, who was backed up against the wall of the house, with three dogs baring their teeth at him. If anything, Clippers, was being more aggressive toward the man than the other dogs, as if she'd had an unfortunate meeting with him before.

And perhaps she had.

When they went back to bed, Brenda simply rolled over and went back to sleep.

Charlotte almost laughed out loud. Porcelain doll, my eye, she thought before she too drifted off to sleep. It was rather a restless sleep, though, because, given her background, her brain was grinding away at all of the possibilities of who did what to who—and why.

First thing the next morning, Charlotte was on the phone to the county sheriff's office. Dave Burch's launching of the two police boats on the Choptank had done the trick. They had zeroed in on the cigarette boat shortly after it had entered the river's mouth on the Chesapeake Bay and had chased it up the river, the chase ending at Charlotte's pier rather than the swamp on the other side of the peninsula. The sheriff hadn't come in to work yet that morning, so Deputy Burch felt free to talk to Charlotte. He knew that no one could process clues and deduce crimes better than she could.

"Yes, there were drugs on the boat. All varieties and a whole boat-load of them." When he realized what he'd said, Burch laughed, and Charlotte joined him, although she felt wound up tight and was apprehensive. "And, yes, they all were in packets with the green palm tree embossed on them. The bad news is that the man in the boat lawyered up before we could get another word out of him. And it was a very, very expensive lawyer. One the New Jersey mob uses. So, this is something big. We just don't know if we'll be able to get anything out of him."

"Damn," Charlotte answered. "I was afraid of that. Did you ID him at all and find out where he's from?"

"Yeah, he's just a small-time hoodlum. Drug connections, though. Lives in the Tidewater area of Virginia. So, he's probably just one mule in a long chain coming up from the south."

"But Madge Miller, who had been dealing in Richmond, was made part of that chain," Charlotte said. "Maybe you should get with the Richmond police and find out if this guy connects there."

"Will do," Burch said. "You going to be around until we wrap this up?"

"I don't know. I doubt it if the only guy you've got is being shut up. Brenda and I are off to Charleston in a week, and that's my priority now. The only other lead we seem to have at the moment is Kurt Clagett. If we could only . . . but let me ring off now, David. There is something I want to check into." She had left Burch with Jason Barnes' number at the Baltimore police. Barnes had agreed to cut through all of the red tape between police departments and to work directly with the Talbot County sheriff's office on the case. If she could do nothing else at this point, Charlotte had thought, this pairing of the two in itself had been quite an accomplishment.

After disconnecting with Burch, Charlotte connected with the administrative office at Curtain Call. She was relieved that the bookkeeper answered rather than Evonne. "Hi, Lacey, it's Charlotte Diamond . . . yes, it sure is a mess, isn't it? There's something I need you to check for me . . . without telling Evonne, if you would. I just don't want to worry her. OK, the staff has to check out when they leave their shifts. I need to know if Kurt Clagett clocked out the night Madge Miller died. Yes, I'll hold." Then after a pause of a few minutes. "He did? 7:00 p.m. Thanks."

That wasn't decisive, of course, she thought. He could have clocked out but stayed around until the times Madge and Walt were killed. She thought for a few minutes and then punched in another number on her cell phone.

She was put through almost immediately to Jason Barnes, chief of the narcotics squad of the Baltimore police. After she'd identified herself and plowed through the preliminaries as politely as she was able, she zeroed in on why she was calling him. "I'm sorry to be calling in the favor this quickly, but this may eventually be as helpful to you as to me.

Have you had a chance yet to work out Kurt Clagett's movements in Baltimore on the night of our murders here? Good. You have any reliable statements on when he first appeared in Baltimore that night? Oh, OK, you say there's a time-dated check-in at his dorm? Thanks. I don't know how it fits in, but we'll keep you posted on that."

When she clicked off, she voiced a low, "Shit," and called David Burch back to pass on what she'd found out and to consult with him on where the investigation needed to go from there. When she looked up from finishing that call, she saw that Brenda was standing near her, leaning on the breakfast bar, and sipping coffee.

Damn, she looks good, Charlotte thought. How can she naturally look so beautiful and I still look like the city dump when I've spent hours primping? Then she laughed. She never spent hours primping.

Brenda wasn't fooled by the laugh. "The case isn't clearing up, is it?" she said.

"No, I'm afraid not. It's getting more complicated."

"I know you don't want it leave it this way," Brenda said. "I'll be happy to go to Spoleto—and Pattie Parker's—by myself."

"Not a chance," Charlotte said. "We're going and we're going together. And we can get a hotel."

"No," Brenda said, with a sigh. "I'm being silly to be wary of Pattie. I've got you to protect me."

"Judging by last night, you could protect us all," Charlotte said.

Then the two of them did laugh a genuine, tension-releasing laugh. Brenda smiled, fully aware of what Charlotte was giving up in her natural inclinations in going to be "just a spouse" while Brenda reveled in the limelight at Spoleto rather than doing what Charlotte was born to do—staying here and solving this damn murder mystery. Perhaps for the first time since they'd said their vows on that snowy night over at Pastor Dunkel's church, Brenda felt that being "just a spouse" was the deepest of commitments to each other.

Chapter Five: Lunch with Evan

Charlotte looked across the front seats of the Jaguar XK-E roadster in as much contentment as one can have who is also digging her nails into the edges of her leather seat in fear. The retired FBI agent found Brenda her most attractive when she was doing her Grace Kelly impersonation, gliding down the highway, looking radiant and oh so cool with round-lens sunglasses and a diaphanous scarf streaming in the wind caused by the high speed of a vehicle with its top down. It was the high speed aspect of the gliding that terrorized the seasoned federal agent.

Brenda often had been compared with Grace Kelly, both box office smash hits in the movies with a sophisticated, calm, intelligent, and timeless blonde beauty. They had played similar roles in the movies, the character stereotype role established by Greer Garson, perpetuated by Grace Kelly, and perfected by Brenda Brandon, which was Brenda Boynton's stage name. The major difference between Grace and Brenda were that Brenda enjoyed a much longer reign and many more awards in the movie business than Grace had. And the other difference, Charlotte mused in her usual self-deprecating style, was that Grace Kelly had married a prince and Brenda had married a toad.

Tough on that, Charlotte quickly thought. She's all mine regardless. Well, mine, and a million movie fans'.

Thinking on the comparison between Grace Kelly and Brenda, though, brought to Charlotte's mind that Grace Kelly had died in an automobile accident combining speed and a winding mountain road, and she reached over and touched Brenda's arm. "I'd like to talk with you a bit about this Pattie Parker we're staying with in Charleston, but you'll probably want to slow down if we are talking."

Thank god the land in this region of Maryland was flat as a table top, Charlotte thought.

The ploy was mostly to get Brenda to slow down, but Charlotte did want to know more about why Brenda was leery about this coming meeting with an actress she had known when she lived in California and how they had hooked up again. She wondered if this Parker woman was behind the invitation for Brenda to perform at Spoleto and if receiving benefit from one of the few people Brenda didn't really like was making Brenda ambivalent about Spoleto when she otherwise would be enthusiastic about it.

The women were driving north on the route 50 dual-lane highway to meet Charlotte's old flame, Evan Worthington, who was the chief of her former FBI office in Annapolis. They were to hook up in Easton, which was roughly half way between Hopewell on the Choptank and Annapolis. Getting Brenda to talk about the coming trip to Charleston to fill in answers to some questions that had been bugging Charlotte would also suffice to blot out Charlotte's worry about meeting Evan again. He had been great about Charlotte marrying Brenda rather than taking up with him again, but Charlotte didn't think she'd ever forget the choice she'd had to make on that and the awkwardness of working with Evan as an FBI consultant. She knew it was not really a hard choice, though, because she was head over heels with Brenda and still in wonder about why Brenda had chosen her.

Charlotte's relationship with Evan had been one of those star-crossed "perfect" matchups that had been defeated by their own immaturity at the time as well as by outside forces. They had both trained at the FBI academy in Quantico, Virginia, and had shared "top of everything" status there. They had naturally fallen into a close, intimate relationship. Charlotte thought of herself—not fully justifiably—as a beached whale body type now, but in those Quantico days even she knew she was in good shape and looking good.

One element they shared, though, was competitiveness, which led to small squabbles and "I'm going to beat you at this" immature contests. These were worried and expanded by another woman, who wanted Evan for herself. Largely because of Charlotte's pride and the difficulty of women to be accepted as equals in the FBI training programs of the time, the other woman won and eventually married Evan. Charlotte, in turn, married on the rebound and definitely got the shorter end of the stick on partners.

Years later, when Charlotte had just retired from the Annapolis office, Even Worthington—not knowing Charlotte had retired—wrangled the office chief position there. His wife had died some years earlier and he'd heard that Charlotte had finally managed to slough off her deadbeat husband, so he had purposely gone after the Annapolis slot to rekindle his relationship with Charlotte. The timing was off, though. By then Charlotte was out of the office and already in a relationship with Brenda. It took a while for Evan to realize that he was no competition for Brenda, which he eventually took well enough, and he had, at least, now managed to bring Charlotte closer again by successfully wheedling her into consulting for the Annapolis office.

As Brenda kept telling Charlotte, investigation was in Charlotte's blood and she would never be content not being able to be involved in that. If Brenda had ever seen the reappearance of Evan Worthington as a threat to her own relationship with Charlotte, she certainly had never shown it. She had welcomed Evan as a mutual friend and conspired with him to return Charlotte to criminal investigation work.

And Brenda had been made aware by Evan that this lunch had some business involved. Otherwise, she and Charlotte might have skipped it. Time was short in their need to be down in Charleston for the start of the Spoleto festival, and Charlotte hadn't placed a high priority on having lunch with Evan before they went. The incentive for her was a conclusion to the drugs and murder case at Curtain Call, and that had been in suspension for several days. There was little likelihood it would be solved before the two women had to travel south. Sheriff Wainwright wasn't being that forthcoming on the progress of the investigation anyway and had pretty much boxed Deputy Burch in from talking to Charlotte about it off the books. Charlotte couldn't really blame the sheriff. The events had happened on the Curtain Call property and, as owners of Curtain Call, Charlotte and Brenda were too close to the investigation to be privy to the prosecution's case. Either or both of them could be classified as suspects; it probably would be pleasing to Wainwright to be able seriously to consider them as such.

"OK, what is it you want us to talk about?" Brenda said as she laughed and shaved ten miles per hour off their progress. "Although I know you just want to get me to slow down. Sorry, I was daydreaming."

"About anything in particular? Maybe about staying with your former colleague down in Charleston?"

"Maybe," Brenda responded.

"Then maybe that's what I want to talk about," Charlotte said. "You've wanted to do Spoleto for years, I know. You have a singing voice that hasn't been showcased enough—your movie success has overshadowed that. But, yet, now that it's happening, you seem reticent about it. I think it has something to do with this Pattie Parker person. I think you should tell me about that before we get down there. What was Pattie Parker to you in the movies? Why are you reluctant to meet her again? Are you afraid she's the one who set up the invitation for you to be at Spoleto, and you worry about her doing that for you? How did you get to be invited to Spoleto this time?"

"My, that's a lot of questions."

"If you drive the speed limit, we have time to cover them all before we get to Easton. Does this Pattie know your orientation and that the spouse you're bringing is female? We really should be straight on that before we get there."

"That's two more questions."

"So perhaps it's time for some of the answers to be coming out."

"I guess you're right," Brenda said with a sigh. When she began to talk, she started at a place that took Charlotte completely by surprise and that had little to do with the questions Charlotte had asked but that did lead into them. "I think what I've been contemplating the most about staying with Pattie Parker while we're in Charleston is the coincidence."

"What coincidence?"

"Madge Miller—not her death necessarily, but her mere existence at a time when Pattie Parker has come back into my life."

"I don't follow."

"Well, as you know, there has to be a movie angle for residents to be accepted at Curtain Call. Madge Miller wasn't accepted either because she owned a movie theater or because she was related to Walt Miller. She was an assistant wardrobe mistress at the studio where I did my last movie, and Pattie Parker also appeared in it. You must remember it. It was *Woman Scorned*, and it paralleled so closely with Helga Lund's murder that suspicion was cast on me and you had to straighten that out when you were in Hollywood."

Helga Lund had been Brenda's older live-in partner when Brenda last lived in Los Angeles. Helga was the costume designer for the movie Brenda had been starring in and had been found hanging from the chandelier in the two-story foyer of Brenda's Hollywood home—murdered in the same way that Brenda's character was under suspicion in the movie for murdering a love affair rival. The police had jumped to the conclusion, as clumsy as the proposition was in real life, that Brenda had acted out in life what she was accused of doing in the movie. It didn't seem to matter to them that the hook of the movie was that Brenda's character hadn't murdered her rival— that she had been framed for the crime.

"Yes I remember that movie and what happened with it."

"You may have been more focused on me than others at the time. But Pattie Parker played the part of the murdered rival, and Madge Miller was an assistant wardrobe mistress on the movie. The two were thick as thieves, and I was subsequently told that one or both of them had given testimony to the police that turned the investigation on me. I didn't really speak with Pattie after that, but I didn't accuse her either. Our relationship was just left in an uncomfortable limbo. I didn't really blame Madge all that much. She isn't what you'd say was a deep thinker, and she obviously didn't like Helga all that much—or, apparently, me."

"And still you let her come to Curtain Call?" Charlotte asked.

"I didn't see any reason to hold that against her. Of course, knowing now what she was involved with here, I probably should have given it a second thought."

"There's no way for you to have known. But, still, I think you do put too much faith in other people sometimes—and you perhaps are too generous. So, it's just this suspicion about Pattie Parker siccing the police on you that has you concerned? I wonder why she'd do that. Well, no, maybe I don't. I had a taste of Hollywood. I can see why a perpetually supporting-role actress would take pains to knock off the leading ladies."

"There's that, of course," Brenda said. "But you might as well know that it goes deeper than that. Pattie Parker liked women too. She had tried for several years to attract me and then, when that didn't work, she tried to put moves on Helga to spite me. The most damning evidence against me at the time was that Helga and I had been quarreling—sometimes in public—for a few weeks before she died. It was Pattie Parker we were quarreling about. It was obvious to me what she was trying to do through Helga. I couldn't make Helga see it that way, though. Helga was fooled. She wasn't romantically drawn to Pattie, but she could only see her as a sweet younger woman who needed a leg up—and Helga was helping to bring her before the studio heads' eyes. The studio heads were hardnosed and not blind about it, but it was starting to redound on Helga."

"And it's that, just that, that has you worried?"

"Yes, that and the coincidence of Madge showing up here in the middle of Pattie's reestablishing contact. Oh, and you asked about the invitation to Spoleto. I don't know fully what that's about. It could have started with Pattie, yes. She lives just outside of Charleston now. She runs a tea plantation in the marshes south of the city, across the Ashley River. But the invitation came from Gordon Galworthy, who is currently the executive director of Spoleto. He was a publicist in Hollywood when I lived there, and I knew him well. I may have told him then that I wanted to do Spoleto some day. Or maybe he's in contact with Pattie down in Charleston and the invitation was initiated by her. I don't know. I hope it was Gordon's idea."

"But you're afraid that Pattie Parker has some scheme on her mind and is going to rear up as a snake in the grass again?"

Brenda didn't respond.

"As I said, you're much too generous with people, Brenda. It's a good thing you told me that. We can just be on our guard now. And, as I said before, we can snub the woman and stay in a Charleston hotel."

"I accepted the invitation to stay with Pattie, and so we'll stay with Pattie—unless, of course, you don't want to. Snubbing isn't my style," Brenda said in a quiet voice.

"I know it isn't. Sometimes I think it should be, though. Far too many take advantage of you. But, we'll leave that for now. I have no objection to staying with this woman as long as I'm permitted to bite back if she bites either one of us. Here we are in Easton. You remember what café we're going to don't you—and that the speed limit here is twenty-five?"

They both laughed.

* * * *

Brenda was always happy when they lunched in Easton, with its colonial, but laid-back, feel and its profusion of antique stores with just the sorts of treasures her own pre-Revolutionary War house was outfitted with. The colonial style she had grown up with had been in sharp contrast with the Malibu modern styles of Hollywood while she lived there, and having had enough of the Hollywood lifestyle made her appreciate the Easton "feel" even more. Charlotte's tastes ran more to the nondemanding "hand-me-down," but she loved to see Brenda beaming, so Easton was just fine with her. She had once preferred Annapolis for its wharf area, but that town had come with her bastard of a husband, Sydney. Charlotte's happiest day spent in Annapolis was the day Sydney ran off with his blonde secretary, Gloria, and became her cross to bear.

Easton was the county seat, where Charlotte and Sheriff Wainwright studiously tried to avoid each other when Charlotte was in town. The town was located on the Tred Avon River and, in many ways, reminded her of an English village, this because it was founded in the eighteenth-century as a fishing village in an English colony deeded by the crown as a Catholic safe haven, most likely to keep that safe haven from being any closer to England proper. It had prospered over the years and now was a gateway to the Maryland, New Jersey, and Delaware eastern seaboard beach resorts. The Tidewater Inn, taking up the center of the town, was a first-class resort for the well-heeled Eastern Shore crowd. But it was the watering hole for so many of these well-heeled patricians that Brenda preferred eating in one of the smaller cafés in the antique store district so that there would be less of a chance she'd be recognized and fussed over.

They had picked Sally's Kitchen, a hole in the wall, on Goldsborough Street today, and they had arrived and been seated just a few minutes before Even Worthington showed up.

Charlotte's heart skipped a beat, as it always did in spite of everything, when she saw him enter the café and move deliberately, every woman's eyes in the place following his progress with approval, toward Charlotte and Brenda's table. The man was aging well, looking perhaps better with graying temples and a bit of meat on his bones than he had looked as a young, wiry FBI agent. His eyes no longer were shielded and looking in every direction for possible danger. He had been "kicked upstairs" and desk bound for nearly a decade now, and his position of authority had straightened his back, broadened his sunny smile, and caused him to walk tall and with confidence, straight at his objective. Still, he was not a dogmatic man. He knew when to veer from the objective when he had to. That's how he'd managed to keep Charlotte as a friend and to add Brenda as one when it became inevitable he'd lose Charlotte to Brenda.

Charlotte and Evan were serious eaters—although neither over ordered—and Brenda was more of a picker and taster, so there wasn't much beyond small talk shared around the table until they were on their coffee and the choice of each from

71

the pastry cart, which was why Sally's Kitchen was chosen for the lunch.

As the waitress moved away with the coffee pot—far enough away so that she didn't overhear them, because Charlotte had caused a coffee pot to hit the floor in this café before by launching into the condition in which she'd found a murdered body the previous day, Charlotte opened up on the Curtain Call investigation.

"Kurt Clagett has melted away from Baltimore," Evan responded in answer to Charlotte's first question. "He disappeared completely—probably the night Madge and Walt Miller died."

"So, he probably was informed of the deaths," Charlotte said. "He was back in Baltimore before the estimated time of death on both of them, but he probably wouldn't have taken off like he did if he didn't know about the deaths."

"Right," Evan responded. "He's probably connected to them then. And he couldn't have just evaporated like that without help, I don't think. You asked me to trace his recent background. He was in Richmond, working for Madge Miller at that theater of hers. And he was on a list of suspects for selling drugs to students at Virginia Commonwealth University and the University of Richmond. VCU was where he got his nurse's training. He was going for a pharmacy degree at Johns Hopkins in Baltimore. His MO, though, is as a dealer to college students. I have no idea how he managed to get into a pharmacy program with drug use and dealing background, let alone be permitted to be within a mile of a college campus. We really must knit police enforcement agency records together better than we do."

"Maybe your next assignment, Evan," Charlotte said, not without enthusiasm. "You were wondering where you could go from here."

"Evonne won't like to hear about the drug dealing," Brenda inserted into the discussion. "But at least she's spared from thinking he could have done the killings. It's been tearing her apart, but, professional that she is, she was back working as always the day after the murders."

Leave it to Brenda to focus on the human element in these situations, Charlotte thought. This was just another reason why she loved the other woman so fiercely. She balanced Charlotte's primary concerns and continually reminded the retired agent that these were people they were dealing with— both good and bad people.

She did have her own focus, though. She turned to Evan and asked, "Was it the same pipeline in Richmond as here and Baltimore?"

"Yes, the same drug signatures and the same packets with the green palm tree embossed on them. The same operation is going on in the Norfolk area and down at Myrtle Beach. We're pushing the inquiries farther south to see how far down it goes—and north as well. These drugs could be getting into Philadelphia, New York, and Boston too. This is a major operation."

"And with a lot of clout if it can pull someone like Kurt Clagett out of circulation so quickly and effectively."

"That's right."

"Is it just up and down the East Coast?"

"We haven't found it to have extended far inland yet," Evan answered.

"So, chances are that the drugs are coming in by sea somehow," Charlotte said.

"Surely not on those cigarette motorboats," Brenda piped up. "Those don't have a great range."

"Yes, probably something with a longer range until they get into a confined region, where they move it by motorboat," Evan said. "They may be pushing in Charleston too. Since you'll be down there, Charlotte—"

"Yes, Evan, I'll keep a look out for evidence down there and call you if—"

"Let me pass on a contact down there for you. Shirley Elgin is the chief of the FBI office down there."

"Shirley Elgin? We've worked together in the past," Charlotte said. She said it tentatively, because she hadn't worked with Elgin with enthusiasm in the past—or received any from Elgin.

"So, I gathered," Evan responded.

"But the FBI office chief for the region? Not a lesser agent?"

"Well, there's something else I was going to ask you to do while you're down there. We'll deputize you and put you on retainer, of course, as it's rather official and important. Maybe a little dangerous too." He was saying all the things he knew would whet an agent's interest in a case. And from the way he was looking at her, Charlotte knew it would be important and unusual—and that this wasn't just a social luncheon. She should have known, she realized, as hard as he had been pushing her to get a luncheon in before she and Brenda left for Charleston.

"OK, I'm intrigued," she answered. She turned and looked at Brenda, who looked suspiciously interested as well.

"There's an unusual possible terrorist or espionage situation at Spoleto," Evan said. "We have others following it, of course, but, since you'll be there anyway, we thought it would be good to have eyes on the inside."

"What sort of situation?"

"There will be a Chinese acrobatic and dance ensemble coming from Beijing to perform at the festival."

"The Temple of Heaven Troupe?" Brenda chimed in. "I've seen them on the schedule. There are more than a dozen of them in the troupe, I think."

"The same, yes," Evan said. Looking back at Charlotte, he continued. "Intelligence is coming to us from inside China that, although they are trained acrobats, some members of the troupe are also nuclear scientists. The intell is garbled. We don't know if they are part of a team to attack a strategic target here or to defect and try to spy long-term for China, or what. But if you can help us figure that out, we'd be grateful. It would be a little hard to believe that a group of Chinese acrobats could also be trained nuclear physicists. And it would give you something more to do than to carry Brenda's cosmetic case while you're there. You and I both know you'll be bored as hell at the festival otherwise."

"You seem to have thought all of this out," Charlotte said.

"I didn't conjure up the possible threat for your enjoyment," Evan said. His voice had a slightly hurt tone to it, but his smile made clear that he was teasing her. "It's just very convenient that you'll be in place."

"I don't know," Charlotte said, although it was obvious to the other two that she was chomping at the bit on the assignment. "What do you think, Brenda?"

Brenda smiled. "Whatever makes you happy, sweetness. But you still would have to attend every one of my performances and applaud and give me wolf whistles. Oh, and you still have to carry my cosmetic case."

On the way back to Hopewell in the Jag, Charlotte said, "You knew about the assignment Evan asked me to take, didn't you? You two ganged up on me."

"It took both of us just to get you to lunch today," Brenda said. There was a hint of laughter in her voice. "And, yes, I knew about it. I was racking my brain to figure out how I could keep you from being bored the next two weeks in Charleston. This is the perfect fix. And, admit it, it's exactly what you want to be doing."

Charlotte refused to admit it—out loud—but she wasn't about to give Brenda an argument on the issue. She already was planning in her mind what she'd have to do to get close to the Chinese acrobatic troupe.

Chapter Six: Welcome to Charleston

"Have you ever been to Charleston before?"

Brenda's question came as a surprise. They had been driving south, on highway 17 along the Atlantic coast, for more than an hour in silence. It was a two-day trip, even at the speeds Brenda tended to drift into, from Maryland to Charleston, and the previous night had been spent in a hi-rise hotel at Myrtle Beach, where Brenda had almost immediately been recognized and swamped by fans. Instead of the dinner they'd planned in a restaurant on the boardwalk, Charlotte went out and brought dinner and a couple of bottles of wine in and they sat on the balcony, watching and listening to the waves roll up onto the beach. Then early to bed—and late to sleep.

It wasn't just the abrupt breaking of the silence that was a surprise, though. What was more surprising was that the question had never come up in all of the preparations for coming to Charleston.

"No," Charlotte answered. "I always wanted to see Charleston, but I never had the opportunity."

"So, I suppose you never got to Savannah either?"

"Alas, no."

"One of my favorite places of all time. So peaceful and quiet—so moving along on Southern time. And all of those small parks, each with its own personality. We must go there someday. I see the two of us sitting on a bench in one of those parks, sitting close, with our arms around each other, and watching the world go by—somewhat like last night. Just the two of us sitting on the balcony of the hotel at Myrtle Beach and watching the waves roll in and then roll out again."

"You aren't going to break into an Otis Redding song, are you?" Charlotte said, and the two women shared a laugh. But Charlotte knew what Brenda meant, and she could easily visualize the mood the actress expressed, as well. "But you're right," she continued. "Last night was heavenly. It was perfect."

"It was nearly perfect," Brenda said, and then she rushed on, "It would have been perfect if Sam and Rocket were along on the trip."

"Amen to that," Charlotte said, the wrench in her heart from the "nearly" word having settled. "We always seem to be leaving those guys when it would be great to take them along." But then she laughed and said, "If we did take them with us, we'd have to take my car and you'd have to cut down on the number of suitcases you need. There's hardly enough room in the backseat of this tin can of yours for the dogs—and you have a suitcase stuffed back there now anyway."

"I've been to Charleston before," Brenda said. "Like New York and San Francisco, it's a great city to be in when you are in love. It's a city for lovers, horse-drawn carriages along a seaside promenade and all."

"You were in love—you were a lover in Charleston?" Charlotte asked, although this always was ground she felt shaky on. She never could quite realize that she wasn't dreaming all of this—that she had wound up with Brenda.

"I was in love. Not a lover, though, which was frustrating, yes, but a long-nursed ache so that I almost missed the ache when it was gone."

"David Runyon?" Charlotte asked in a voice so low that Brenda had to incline her head toward her partner and Charlotte had to repeat what she had said. Runyon had been Brenda's perpetual leading man in a series of highly popular films, popular because of the easy, both comedic and romantic, chemistry between the two on the silver screen. Brenda had pined for years, she had said, for something with Runyon in their personal lives that would approach what they had together on the screen.

"Yes, it was with David. We were filming a movie in Charleston—some pre-Civil War hoop skirt historical. I was as mad for David then as I ever was. He looked so handsome in a Confederate uniform, ready to march off to war. The movie ended with the firing on Fort Sumter—it's right there in Charleston, you know, out in Charleston Harbor, the shot that kicked off the Civil War. It was the first of two movies that went together. That one ended in chaos and the shattering of the world our two characters were in—and falling deeply in love. The second movie was set further inland, after the war, after both of our characters had been hardened and disillusioned. That was one of coming together with eyes more open, more humbled, and establishing a more realistic basis in their relationship."

"So they married and lived happily ever after?"

"In the movie series? No, they ended up each married to someone else—but, yes, happily, I think."

After a long pause, Charlotte asked the burning question. "And you and David Runyon?"

"It took several more movies together, but I think it was those two movies here in Charleston that opened my eyes to reality—although, open or not, I didn't see it for several more years. It was Russel Rines. In the first of those two movies."

"Ah," Charlotte said, knowing what was coming.

"Russel Rines, the supporting male lead, looked as good—maybe better than David did in a Confederate uniform. David seemed to think so too. I'm sure I knew then, but I went on for several more years thinking that David would eventually change. But of course he didn't. And to think that years later, I myself . . ."

Another long pause, as Charlotte watched the Arthur Ravenel Jr. Bridge across the Cooper River into the heart of the city of Charleston materialize in the distance and grow larger in her sight. "And do you regret—?"

"There's always a twinge of something, of course. It would not have been real if there wasn't. And my pining was certainly real. But, no, I'm relieved. I got the best of all worlds in the end. I got you."

The two women didn't speak again, each lost in their own reverie, as the bridge loomed ahead of them and then was under the wheels of the Jaguar.

"We each have someone to meet here in Charleston before pressing ahead to the tea plantation—me with Gordon Galworthy and you with the FBI chief here. Should we split up?"

"No, I don't want to split up," Charlotte said. After what they'd discussed, how could she want to separate even for a minute from Brenda? "We'll take them consecutively. You first."

Always you first, Charlotte thought, all aglow again with the knowledge that Brenda was hers.

* * * *

The offices of the Spoleto Festival were on George Street in the heart of the College of Charleston, which itself was in the heart of the city. Most venues for the springtime festival were in college performance halls. The festival of music and performance art was founded in this same venue in 1977 as the counterpart in America to the Festival dei Due Mondi—the Festival of Two Worlds—that was founded in the late 1950s in Spoleto, Italy, by the Pulitzer Prize-winning composer, Gian Carlo Menotti.

The festival provides an eclectic schedule of music, dance, theater, opera, and visual arts. Most performances being by talented, rising stars in their field, with an emphasis on academic training. Occasionally, as in the case of Brenda Brandon—Brenda Boynton's stage name—major performers are invited. But, as was the case with Brenda, they were invited to showcase a talent that wasn't what they were well known for. Brenda was a movie star, but she was also an accomplished torch singer, and this was the capacity in which she had received the invitation. And the man they went to the offices of the festival to meet, Gordon Galworthy, made quite clear when they arrived in his office that he had been the one to formulate the invitation.

"I know you are going to surprise a whole lot of people, Brenda," he said as he met them at the door. "There are only a few, I think, who know you are a singer. Next year perhaps we'll invite you to dance." There was a twinkle in the eye of his dapper and distinguished English gentleman countenance when he said that. Brenda indeed had trained as a dancer as well as an actress and singer, but what few knew was that in her era, a performer had to be accomplished in all to rise in the industry.

"Now, Gordie, you've known me so long that you know I'm far too old to kick up my heels anymore."

"You are ageless and looking even more lovely now than when you were in Hollywood," Galworthy gushed as he leaned over and kissed her hand. "When I took this position with the festival, I told them that I would only take it if I could sign one personal favorite performance each year. You were my first pick."

That seemed to settle whether he or Pattie Parker had been the source of the invitation.

He was gushing, but it occurred to Charlotte as he graciously received the introduction of her as Brenda's spouse that his joy at meeting with Brenda again was genuine, as was her affection for him. Brenda had filled Charlotte in on their connection—Galworthy had been the publicist for Brenda's movie studio and he had been her staunchest supporter and friend when she was under suspicion for having murdered Helga Lund. Charlotte could also see, though, that he was one smooth operator, which, she supposed, he would have had to be to survive as a top-drawer publicist in California.

Once they were settled in his office, Galworthy got right to business. "I hope you don't mind being in the Cistern Yard. It's the center of the campus here and it's where all of the small jazz ensembles are performing. It's in the open air, but you have just four performances spread over the seventeen-day festival and the night air is warm this time of year in Charleston. We have the nearby Simons Center recital hall reserved in case it needs to be moved indoors."

"That would be fine," Brenda answered, "and I must thank you for bringing the Joey Bent Jazz Quartet in to back me up."

"That's who I first heard you sing with," Galworthy said. "I won't ever forget that performance—I had had no idea you had such a divine voice. I wanted to recreate that."

"I noticed," Brenda said, with a laugh. "It's what you put in the publicity."

"And of course you'll be coming to the opening and closing banquets, I hope. The opening is tonight at 8:00 at the Simons Center. I talked with Pattie Parker, and she said she'd see that you got here."

"Yes, we'll be here," Brenda answered.

Galworthy turned his full attention to Charlotte then, although he had been deftly including her in the discussion all along. "And are you a singer too, Ms. Diamond?"

"I can sing as well as any toad could," she answered with a laugh. "And I do thank you for not asking about dance. No, I'm not in entertainment. I'm just a retired public servant."

"But certainly you are one who is interested in the arts," he said, with an amused expression on his face.

"I'm interested in an artist, Brenda. And I'm interested in any art Brenda is engaged in," she replied.

"It's a two-week festival. I certainly hope there will be other performances we can tempt you with."

"As a matter-of-fact, I am very interested in the Chinese acrobatic troupe that's performing—the Temple of Heaven Troupe, I think they're called."

"Ah, yes. They'll be performing at the Memminger Auditorium on Beaufain Street. We'll have to get you there to see them—and a backstage pass to meet them if you like."

"Yes, I would like that. The first available performance that's possible."

"They may be at the banquet tonight—at least the troupe leaders. We'll have to get you together with them."

The prospect of getting close to the troupe was turning out to be much more simple than Charlotte had dreamed it would be.

The second meeting didn't go quite so well or smoothly. The FBI office was in a more commercial, less historical part of town a few blocks south of the college. They left the Jag in the

86

parking space Galworthy had arranged for them in one of the college's garages and walked the few blocks to the FBI office.

The historical and classic Charleston side-entrance residential style of architecture and ambiance of the city had a split personality. Charleston was on an oblong peninsula that came to a point in Charleston Harbor, which opened into the Atlantic. Since the founding of the city, the peninsula had been split more or less by King Street, running down the center of the peninsula to its tip. From a couple of blocks to the south of this street and running north to the shores of the Cooper River was the wealthy section of town. The historical mansions, shops, and churches on this side of the city had continually been renewed despite fire, flood, the effects of the Civil War and hurricane. The workers serving the wealthy through history resided mostly to the south of King Street, toward the Ashley River. Restoration had rarely occurred here, so that this side of town was both more run down than the other and had newer construction and architecture.

The FBI office was in a nondescript concrete block of 1950s-style architecture four blocks south of the College of Charleston campus on Bull Street. The offices were on the top floor of a four-story building and had the security of a fortress. They were cold, austere, and all business. And so, when the office chief and head agent came out to the waiting room to receive Charlotte, was Special Agent Shirley Elgin.

Seeing the woman approach, Charlotte had risen from her chair beside Brenda in the waiting room and had advanced to meet her. She'd already covered with Brenda that the actress would probably have to wait in the waiting room, as there would be classified or proprietary FBI business to be discussed, and Brenda was fine with that. When Elgin came into the room, she was focused on Charlotte, so she didn't even see Brenda.

Charlotte didn't like the cold stare on the special agent's face. The two were acquainted from various FBI meetings they both had attended, but they had not interacted enough to call themselves friends. And today, although Charlotte couldn't place it right away, there seemed to be hostility just under the other woman's surface. She was polite, but just barely, and she wasn't exactly forthcoming on the possible defection case Charlotte was there to coordinate on. Elgin only reluctantly deputized Charlotte so she could take action, as appropriate, on the possible terrorism case, even though Evan Worthington had told Charlotte that wouldn't be a problem.

It didn't take long during the conversation for Charlotte to get the impression that Agent Elgin hadn't been pleased by having a retired agent—even one with the sterling reputation Charlotte had—being inserted on her turf.

"We've been preparing for this Spoleto case for months," Elgin said early in the discussion. "I'm always pleased to accommodate a request from Agent Worthington in Annapolis, but I do hope you won't do anything to jeopardize plans and preparations we've already made. We don't really need more analysis from a remove. The only help we would have any use for would be if we could place someone—"

"We've just been from a meeting with the executive director of the festival," Charlotte said. "He's arranging for me to meet the leaders of the Chinese troupe tonight at a banquet, and I'll be attending their first performance the day after tomorrow—with a backstage pass to meet and talk with the entire troupe. And, no, I didn't tell the festival official that I had any more interest in the troupe than just that, artistic interest."

"Oh," Agent Elgin answered, "that would have been Gordon Galworthy." Charlotte just nodded in agreement. Clearly she was already in a position to provide the only help Elgin was saying her office might need. But clearly also, the special agent still didn't like the idea of Charlotte's presence in her case.

"Where are you staying in Charleston—in case we need to contact you?" she asked.

"I'll be at the Palmetto Tea Plantation out on Wadmalaw Island. With Pattie Parker."

"The tea plantation? Pattie Parker?" Obviously this had gotten the special agent's attention and surprised her. She started to say something but then clammed up.

And that's the impression that Charlotte clearly was getting. The woman had information to share on her operations but wasn't going to tell Charlotte any more than she minimally had to. The inference was clear that Charlotte wasn't wanted on Shirley Elgin's turf.

But at the end of the meeting, the woman started to thaw a bit—and the realization hit Charlotte that she had been quite wrong about the reason for the freeze.

As they rose to leave the office, Elgin said, "You're consulting for Evan Worthington now, aren't you?"

"Yes, but only infrequently," Charlotte asked.

"The rumor is that you two are a pair again. Is it wise for you to be working in the same office?"

By now they had reached the waiting room, and the real reason for Shirley Elgin's iciness was dawning on Charlotte. She gestured for Brenda to rise and step forward. As Elgin's eyes focused on Brenda, her jaw dropped in recognition of the movie star.

"The rumors are off," Charlotte said sweetly. "Evan and I are just friends and colleagues. I'm married now. And I'd like you to meet my wife, Brenda Boynton. I think you recognize her as Brenda Brandon, though."

They left the office before Shirley Elgin lifted her jaw off the floor. She might be resisting an agent of Charlotte's reputation being inserted in her operation, but having mentioned rumors going around the FBI community, Charlotte now remembered the rumor that Shirley Elgin had a crush of her own on Evan Worthington. Charlotte could see now that Elgin had seen her as competition in that quarter—but Charlotte hoped that fear had now been dispelled.

They walked back to the college campus, but as they entered the parking garage, Charlotte froze for a moment and then asked Brenda to go ahead and get into the Jag—but to excuse her for a few moments as she had a call to make.

She exited the garage, turned into a side street, and punched a number into her cell phone.

"Evonne? It's me, Charlotte. Brenda and I are down in Charleston and I just wanted to check with you on how things are going at Curtain Call—and about anything happening with the investigation." She listened for a few minutes and then, as casually as she could, asked, "And the staff? Everyone has stayed on in spite of the two murders? Oh, she did? Well, I hope you are able to find a replacement quickly. Oh, you did already? Efficient as always, Evonne. We'll call and check in again in a couple of days. You have our phone number at the tea plantation, don't you, and our cell phone numbers? Good."

When she clicked off, she quickly made two more calls. One was to Sheriff Wainwright's office, happily finding Deputy Burch on duty and Wainwright not. The second call went to Jason Barnes, the chief of narcotics of the Baltimore police. She half thought of giving Shirley Elgin a call but decided that she could hear it through official channels. Perhaps if she'd been more forthcoming with Charlotte . . .

"You were gone long enough to make several calls," Brenda said when Charlotte returned to the car.

"Which, in fact, I did."

"Important calls?"

"I think you can say that. I guess you didn't see that couple getting into the car at the other end of the garage when we came in."

"No, I didn't. Someone you recognized?"

"I think so, but I can't be positive. Seeing them both, together, though, makes it more likely."

"Seeing who?"

"Kurt Clagett and Nurse Annie—Annie Nusbaum. My first call was to Evonne. Annie resigned the other day and cleared out. She said she couldn't get over having Madge Miller die under her care. But it looks perhaps like she was absconding because she was doing more than just nursing at Curtain Call. It looks like this might be where Kurt Clagett—and Annie—were sent by the drug operation to get them out of the clutches of the Maryland authorities. And I'll just bet that if the authorities look around on this campus they'll find some of those little plastic packets with the green palm tree embossed on them."

Brenda whistled. "Talk about coincidences."

"That's the biggest reason for me not to be sure about what I thought I saw," Charlotte answered in a contemplative tone. "I don't believe in coincidences."

Chapter Seven: Tea or Me?

Although Wadmalaw Island, the location of the Palmetto Tea Plantation, was only about twenty-five miles south of Charleston by road, it was a fast trip into seemingly untamed rural marsh and the life of an earlier century. The island was accessible from highway 17 south of Charleston solely by the two-lane Maybank highway, with the only island road access being across Church Creek. The plantation itself was at the end of the island, separated from the Atlantic by a narrow strip of marshland and screened from the sea by palmetto trees. The mix of the sandy soil and just the right amount of average rainfall made the island the only place in the United States where tea cultivation was being attempted.

Brenda had no idea how Pattie Parker had made it here. She only knew that something had happened within the movie studio when Brenda had moved away from Hollywood that no one would talk about that had stopped the movie scripts coming Pattie's way. She did an occasional TV series appearance now and a few commercials for products that indicated she didn't have much of a choice on the film work she accepted.

"How exactly did Pattie Parker learn that you were coming to Spoleto?" Charlotte asked as they drove out of Charleston and onto Wadmalaw Island after the meetings with the Spoleto executive director and the Charleston FBI chief agent.

"I'm not sure," Brenda answered. "I think she is on one or more of the Spoleto planning committees. She must have heard it there."

For some reason it was nagging at Charlotte that she really needed to check that out. There was something odd about Parker agreeing to the invitation being offered when it didn't seem like she was the least bit friendly toward Brenda when they previously knew each other—certainly not if she had been the source of rumors implicating Brenda as a murderess. Charlotte had asked Gordon Galworthy about that, but the subject had been changed before she was fully satisfied that Parker had had nothing to do with the invitation and he'd left the inference that it was wholly his idea.

The private road to the plantation house, which indeed was an old pre-Civil War plantation house that was still in the process of being renovated, led through a corner of the tea plantation, where the tea plants were laid out in hedgerows with grass lanes between them. The hedges were some four feet high, and, as Brenda concentrated on navigating the narrow, sandy drive with pot holes that presented a serious challenge to her low-slung Jaguar, Charlotte noted the unusual piece of machinery that seemed to be harvesting tea leaves. It was a big-wheeled tractor-like affair with a truck bed behind it. It hovered over a hedge line, with its wheels driving along the grassy lanes on either side of the hedges, and after it passed a section of the hedge, the planting was nearly the same height as before the contraption drove over it.

"I wonder what that machine is doing," Charlotte said.

Brenda paused the Jaguar and looked out into the field. "That's the tea harvester," she answered. "It's just cutting the very new growth and sending it back into the truck bed behind. In the tea plant, those will be the tea leaves that are being processed. Most of the bush won't be touched."

"How did you know that?"

"I read about the process as soon as I got the invitation. I had no idea there was a tea plantation in the States. The difference between this operation and anything in India or Sri

Lanka is the cost of labor. The people who sold this place to Pattie had to figure out how to harvest by machine. In India they can afford to harvest by hand, but not here. It is grueling, and time-consuming work to do it by hand. Not cost effective here. As it is, I wonder how Pattie can get a profit out of this."

"Maybe she subsidizes it with her film earnings."

"Have you seen the commercials she's in? I doubt there's much profit in those."

"Point taken," Charlotte answered. And then they were pulling up in front of the plantation house, and a woman was coming out of the front door, having heard the purring motor of the Jaguar approaching. At first she didn't look like a woman. She was dressed in men's work clothes and had a short-cropped head of black hair.

"Pattie Parker?" Charlotte asked uncertainly. It didn't look like the woman she'd seen in commercials, who had appeared quite feminine.

"Not on your life," Brenda answered, with a husky laugh. "Pattie is partial to flowing red tresses—and wouldn't, I think, be seen dead in masculine clothing—unless a film part demanded it."

And, indeed, it wasn't Pattie Parker who was the first to greet them.

"Hello, I'm Regina Quinn, Pattie Parker's sometimes personal assistant. And you must be Brenda Brandon. I've seen your movies, of course." The woman moved directly down the steps and over to Brenda's side of the Jag, barely giving Brenda time to get out of the vehicle before Regina had Brenda's hand in a firm grip and was leaning into her—almost eating her up would have been Charlotte's description. She had moved down to the car in a man's gait. Charlotte, of course, seemed not even to be there to her. All of her attention went to Brenda.

In contrast, Pattie Parker herself was the next to come out of the house. The contrast was partially in looks. She was all feminine demeanor and movement—a striking redhead apparently in her middle forties, all frills and cosmetics and girlish giggles. The other contrast was that she fairly flowed down the stairs and, although giving a greeting to Brenda in passing, made directly for Charlotte, just now huffing out of the confining space and low-slung seat of the roadster.

"And who is this darling woman?" Pattie gushed. "Is this your new partner, Brenda? It must be. So . . . statuesque and interesting looking."

Nice turn of a phrase for lumbering and elephantine, Charlotte thought, as Pattie patted her all over and made Charlotte feel she had fallen into a cotton candy machine.

"Charlotte's my wife," Brenda answered. "Charlotte Diamond. Charlotte, meet Pattie Parker, the movie actress, and Regina Quinn, is it? I'm happy to meet you."

"Are you connected with the movies too, Charlotte?" Pattie asked. "I don't remember meeting you out in Hollywood, and I think I would remember such a strikingly intelligent and handsome woman as you." If Charlotte didn't know better, she would have thought the woman was trying to put the moves on her. Pattie certainly was beautiful enough—still—to be very attractive.

"Charlotte's a retired senior FBI agent," Brenda said. "We met in Maryland after I moved back to my home town there. She's the mayor of that town too. I surprised you don't remember her from Hollywood. She's the one who cleared me of the charges of killing Helga."

Charlotte could feel Pattie stiffen—which went to her facial muscles too—but her face recovered more quickly than the hands she had been patting Charlotte with. "By a Maryland town, You mean Hopewell, where you own the rest home?"

"Yes, Charlotte's my partner in owning Curtain Call."

Interesting, Charlotte thought, that Hopewell and the rest home could come into Pattie Parker's mind so quickly, bloating out the mention of Hollywood and the murder investigation. She otherwise had instantly come across as incredibly self-absorbed. There also was something fishy about the fawning attention she was devoting to Brenda's partner— almost as if she was sending a message of challenge to Brenda. Perhaps the games were beginning, Charlotte thought.

"It was nice meeting you . . . both," Regina said, "But I have to get to my real job now." Pattie's assistant had belatedly included Charlotte, but she still only had eyes for Brenda and hadn't let loose of her yet. The flip side of the game? Charlotte wondered. Or was the obviously butch woman sending genuine personal signals of her own to Brenda?

"Your real job?" Brenda asked.

"I have a charter fishing and tourist excursion boat. I keep it here, but I run it out of Charleston for tourists. You can see it out there on the water."

Brenda and Charlotte turned their eyes toward where Regina was gesturing and sure enough, through a thin stand of palmetto trees, there was the Atlantic. There also was a long pier, with several row and motorboats tied to it and out in the sea not only the fishing boat Regina referred to but also a float plane.

"Is the plane yours too?" Charlotte asked.

"No," Pattie answered before Regina could. "That's Cameron's. My husband's. He's also into charter, but by air rather than a fishing boat. There he is on the pier. He should be up here in a few minutes."

Her husband? Charlotte thought—and she could see that Brenda had the same thought. Charlotte had gotten the distinct impression that Pattie was an avowed lesbian. Charlotte had already decided that she was probably paired off with Regina. Well, well, well.

As the man approached the house, though, she had the impression that this was yet another part of a game by Pattie to somehow attack Brenda. The man was a dead ringer for the actor David Runyon—Brenda's perpetual leading man and the man Brenda had waited for unrequitedly for decades—but at an earlier age by decades than Runyon had been when he died. Looking at Brenda, Charlotte could see that she was struck with the resemblance as well, and the twitching of the corner of the actress' mouth told Charlotte that the barb—because surely it was a purposeful barb—had struck home.

Cameron Reed was appropriately introduced to both women and, although gruff in a rough-edged man of adventure way, was nothing close to as refined as Gordon Galworthy had been earlier that afternoon, Charlotte got the impression that he had no idea that he was being cast in the role of David Runyon in whatever game Pattie was playing.

"Glad to have met you," he said, not giving Brenda any more attention than he gave Charlotte—for which Charlotte was extremely grateful, knowing how affected Brenda was at seeing him, "and I trust we will have longer to talk at the Spoleto opening banquet tonight—Pattie has roped me into going and wearing a monkey suit to boot—but I phoned Jose from the plane to come pick me up. One of the sorting machines isn't properly sorting. It's always something in an operation like this."

"Cam pulls maintenance on all of our machinery," Pattie said, putting her arm through his and giving Brenda a "he's all mine" sweet smile. "It's so handy to have a man around the place."

As she was saying this, a white SUV was pulling in to the parking circle in front of the house. A young Hispanic man was at the wheel. The referenced Jose, Charlotte assumed. But then her eyes went to the business logo on the passenger door of the SUV and she froze. It was of a palm branch, painted in green.

"That logo," she involuntarily said out loud.

"It's a saw palmetto branch," Regina Quinn said. "We're the Palmetto Tea Plantation. The palmetto is the state tree of South Carolina, you know."

"Yes, I know," Charlotte said pensively. She knew that it would just be a coincidence that the green logo on the drug packets she'd seen was something more like a date palm. But these pesky coincidences. Perhaps it was just a coincidence that Cameron Reed was a dead ringer for a young David Runyon too—but Charlotte didn't really believe in coincidences.

"Would either of you like to ride over to the plant with us and take a look at the operation?" Reed politely asked.

"That's more Charlotte's thing than mine," Brenda said. "Perhaps I can get us unpacked and have a chance to go over the songs I plan to sing at Spoleto—and Charlotte could take the tour. She could tell me what she saw."

"Yes, I would like that," Charlotte said. She was thinking that it would give her a chance to quiz Reed more directly—although she couldn't presently think of what she should quiz him about.

However, Reed parted with Charlotte and Jose at the processing plant after having given Charlotte a brief tour of that, saying he knew what the sorting machine needed, but that it needed it before they could start up the line again. He told Jose, a nice-looking young man who was introduced to Charlotte as Jose Almirez—a third-generation American Hispanic, Reed made sure Charlotte knew, as Charlotte's FBI past had been revealed to him—to give her the tour of the fields and outlying buildings.

It was in another building, rectangular and made of cinderblocks, one of two identical buildings side by side, that Charlotte got her second jolt. Jose was taking her through the packaging process when she saw them—boxes and boxes of packets, all with the same green palm tree embossed on them as the drug packets that she'd seen in Maryland.

"What are these?" she asked sharply.

Was that a guarded look Jose gave her before he answered?

"That's what we package the individual servings of tea in. That's the company logo."

"Not exactly. Not the same palm tree. Do you make these yourself here?"

"No. Regina orders them from a company. Down in Florida, I think."

Another one of those pesky coincidences, Charlotte thought.

"Can you get me the name of the company you use, Jose?" Charlotte asked.

"Regina could tell you."

"Yes, I'm sure she could. But could you get the name without telling Regina I've asked for it?"

"Yes, ma'am, if you want," Jose answered. He gave her a guarded look, but Charlotte didn't give him an explanation. "I can maybe get it for you tomorrow."

As they left that building, Charlotte walked over to the door of the adjacent building, which was a duplicate of the first, expecting to get a tour of that, as well, but Jose headed for the vehicle. Turning, he said, "That's just another packaging building. Just a duplicate of this one for when the harvest is at its peak."

Charlotte had thought that the harvesting was an ongoing process without a peak season, but she decided that she just must have misunderstood that information.

When Jose took Charlotte back to the house, she found Brenda in their shared bedroom, looking pale. Charlotte thought she knew why, and what Brenda said first bore out her hunch.

"He looks just like David once did," she said.

"I know," Charlotte answered. "And it isn't lost on me that Regina is making up to you and Pattie is making up to me. Divide and conquer, I presume. I don't think Pattie offered us room and board here during Spoleto to be friendly. I think she's trying to upset you."

"I hope it's only that," Brenda said.

"What do you mean?"

"While you were gone, she took me on a tour of the house, including the section that's still be renovated. The floors aren't all back in over there and I almost fell two stories into the basement."

"That's terrible," Charlotte said, sitting down on the bed next to Brenda and drawing the woman into her embrace, "So that's why you look pale. It isn't because Pattie's husband is the spitting image of David."

"Well, it's probably a combination of the two. The worst thing, though, is that when I almost tripped and fell, I could have sworn that Pattie was pushing me from behind."

"That settles it," Charlotte said. "We're going back into town and finding a hotel."

"There really isn't time today. We have to get ready for the banquet now and I've already unpacked our things. Let's talk about it in the morning."

"Let's more than talk about it in the morning," Charlotte said. "We'll do some repacking while we dress for dinner. First thing tomorrow we're out of here. That Pattie Parker is out to get you, and I plan on finding out why."

"Maybe then we should stay," Brenda said, her voice sounding stronger now. "This is the best place to uncover what that is."

* * * *

It seemed like all of the glitterati of Charleston—which included many well-heeled Southern aristocrats indeed—turned out for the opening banquet for the Spoleto Festival that evening, and Brenda's party was seated prominently in the center of it all. Brenda was pretty much the centerpiece performer for the festival. She and Charlotte, along with Pattie Parker and Cameron Reed, were seated at the head table with Gordon Galworthy and the major financial backers of the festival.

Throughout the evening other prominent people drifted by to be introduced to Brenda. She hardly got a bite to eat, but she—along with Pattie Parker—was accustomed to this, and a snack had been prepared for their party at the plantation house before they'd driven into Charleston.

Pattie didn't stay at the table, no doubt not wanting to be in Brenda's shadow there. She mingled with the diners in the hall, and, being a vivacious and curvaceous redhead of great beauty and familiarity on the TV screen—even if people couldn't quite remember what they'd seen her in on the TV screen—she was continually in a swirl of people—mostly men—and in her element.

Cameron Reed most definitely was not in his element, however. Throughout the early part of the night he appeared more as a paid escort for Pattie, coming into play only when she wanted him to—which wasn't often. As soon as he'd eaten, and heartily so despite the earlier snack he'd had, he permitted a couple of the other men who also appeared not to want to be there to entice him to go on an expedition in the rambling Simmons Arts building to fight boredom. It was later revealed that they'd found a games room—pool and ping pong—in the dressing room area of the stage theater complex and untied their formal bow ties, broke out their cigars, picked up pool cues, and found their own way to enjoy the banquet.

A long table near the entrance of the dining room had been given over to the Chinese acrobatic troupe, most of whom were clinging close together and watching the elegant swirl of pampered people in evening clothes jabbering merrily and boisterously as they moved through the room. Charlotte looked over at their table, wishing she had the opportunity to begin assessing the potential danger of the group as Evan had asked her to do. As if he had divined her need, Gordon Galworthy turned to her. "You have spied our Chinese acrobats, I see. Would you like to meet them?"

"I most certainly would. Their art fascinates me."

Gordon took her over to the edge of the table, where three of the members of the troupe watched her approach— each with different expressions. The young woman Gordon introduced Charlotte to first, who was named Li Fen, was all bubbly smiles. She received the first introduction because she spoke English well and apparently was the troupe translator. Beside her, and leaning into her somewhat possessively, was a young man whose eyes were alive with interest to converse with an American, which he did in halting English, helped by Li Fen. He said his name was Huang Bao.

The third man, who merely stiffly nodded his head when introduced as Feng Da, was older. He didn't appear to Charlotte to be as prepared to do somersaults around the room as most of the others at the table were, and her deduction proved to be correct. Gordon indentified him as the troupe leader and, he said, security officer, which told Charlotte all she needed to know about the man with the eyes that looked dead and yet took everything in at the same time. He, to put it bluntly, was the troupe's jailer and disciplinarian.

A couple of other members of the troupe hovered around the periphery, showing interest, but not speaking. A middle-aged woman was identified as the troupe's wardrobe mistress, and a very fit-looking, slim young man seemed to follow the conversation so well that Charlotte suspected that he also was proficient in English. But he didn't comment during the discussion.

Charlotte sat talking with the younger pair for a few minutes, her mind racing to try to visualize them as industrial spies. But if they were, they were also consummate actors. Li Fen did most of the talking on their side. She remained bubbly, but Charlotte could also discern that she was weighing her words when she spoke and for a reason beyond the difficulty of navigating the language barrier. Feng Da was hovering over her shoulder. Charlotte wondered how much English he could understand.

"We have been so much looking forward to visiting your country," Li Fen said. At her side, holding her hand, the handsome young Huang Bao wagged his head in agreement. "This is a lovely city. So exotic."

Charlotte almost chuckled at the different perspective displayed—that Charleston would be seen as exotic by someone from the Orient.

"You must explore the city while you're here," Charlotte said. "You really must get down to the tip of the peninsula, to Battery Park, where you can see the ocean across Charleston Harbor."

"That would be so nice," Li Fen said, but with a tone regret in her voice, she said, "But I'm afraid we will not have the time or opportunity for this."

Feng Da had a hand on the young woman's elbow, and Li Fen winced slightly as if he had applied pressure.

"Well, I'll talk with Gordon Galworthy, the festival director, and we'll see what we can work out with your troupe leaders. It would be a shame to come this far without seeing more of America." And then, because time was of the essence and she sensed she wouldn't have many opportunities, she added, "But perhaps you or Huang Bao here might wish to come live in America some day."

This elicited a different and more dramatic response than Charlotte expected—beyond the slight hiss she thought she heard escape Feng Da's compressed lips. Li Fen looked surprised and almost frightened. "Oh, I would never wish to live anywhere but China," she said.

Charlotte looked over at Huang Bao, who looked a bit less shocked at the suggestion.

She would have liked to have pursued the point, still trying to slash right down to whether these people were actually nuclear scientists and spies, but she sensed Feng Da tensing and starting to rise from his seat.

In the moment before he was able to cut the discussion to a close, though, Huang Bao hugged Li Fen closer and piped up to say, "We have dreamed of regular visits to your Las Vegas. We understand that our art is popular there, but China is our home."

Feng Da's rising to his feet marked the end of the discussion, and Charlotte departed as graciously as she felt able. As she moved toward the head table, though, she had two impressions. First, that Huang Bao was trying to defuse a tongue lashing of Li Fen when the troupe returned to their accommodations—he was affirming in the security officer's mind Li Fen's answer that she wouldn't want to live anywhere but China—and that, because periodic trips to Las Vegas were the first things that had sprung to his mind, he either was very clever or very focused on acrobatic performance.

At the head table Charlotte found herself sitting next to Gordon Galworthy again, and when there was a break in the people coming by to greet him and to hope for an introduction to Brenda, she found an opportunity to quiz him further on the invitations sent to Brenda.

"So, Gordon, when Brenda accepted the invitation to perform, I take it you arranged with Pattie Parker to invite us to stay with her."

"Oh, no. Pattie Parker knew she had been invited and more or less told me that Brenda would be staying with her. We'd already made arrangements for Brenda and you to stay with the college president. His house is right here in the center of the campus. It would have been quite convenient to all of the festival venues."

"We may be taking you up on that offer if it remains in play—or arranging for a hotel room in town."

He didn't seem surprised and said so. "I'm sure the president would still love to host you, if you wish. I'll admit I was surprised when Pattie said Brenda would be staying with her. It was no secret that relations between the two were, shall we say, a bit stiff in Hollywood. In fact. I was surprised when Pattie came up with Brenda's name as a possible festival headliner in an early planning meeting."

"I thought you said inviting Brenda was your idea."

"I had certainly dreamed of doing so, and I sent the invitation, but Pattie mentioned it first. I was surprised by that."

And well you should have been, Charlotte thought. That cleared up something she hadn't understood. She was about to follow that up with another question when she looked across the room to find a late-appearing couple at the entrance into the banquet hall and, in spite of how she had thought she'd react to such a sighting, her heart beat faster and then almost stopped.

Standing in the doorway was the chief of the Charleston FBI office, Shirley Elgin. Her arm was laced with that of the chief of the Annapolis FBI office, Evan Worthington. Shirley looked like she was in seventh heaven. She also had cleaned up very nicely—and Evan, as always, was looking gorgeous.

Evan was looking around the room. He spotted Charlotte and, after being accompanied to empty chairs at a table and getting Shirley settled, he sought Charlotte out.

"What a surprise seeing you here. I didn't know you'd be coming to Charleston," Charlotte said as he approached her. She hoped that her voice didn't sound icy, but she was afraid that it did.

"I didn't know I was coming, either, Charlotte. Something has come up. I need to talk to you, and I need you and Brenda—"

"And who is this gorgeous hunk you've been keeping from me, Charlotte sweetie?"

It was Pattie Parker, arriving back at the table—or weaving back to the table. And Cameron Reed was returning as

111

well, from another direction. Pattie had obviously had several cocktails during her wandering.

"This is Evan Worthington," Charlotte said. "He's—"

"Just a business acquaintance of Charlotte and Brenda's from up North," Evan interjected. He turned his face to Charlotte and gave her a piercing look that signaled he didn't want his FBI affiliation known. Used to the maneuver, Charlotte caught on quickly.

"Well, as much as I'd like to stick around and get to know you better, Mr. Worthington," Pattie said, slurring her words, "this little girl is more than a little tipsy, and it's time for her to be going home."

There was a bustling at the table with the Parker party, including a tired-looking Brenda, saying their farewells, and then they were leaving.

Charlotte didn't really want to talk to Evan under the circumstances. She needed time to adjust to the surprising and, she knew, unwarranted jealously that had screamed into her brain at the sight of Evan and Shirley together. Anyone but Shirley, she was thinking. But in the surprised and shocked state she was in, she couldn't be sure that she believed that it just was because it was Shirley Elgin.

"We have to talk, Charlotte. First thing in the morning. I'll call you on your cell phone."

"If you like, Evan." Now she knew she'd used an icy tone. And she could kick herself. She had no claim on Evan. She'd given up any claim she might have.

More ashamed now than mad, she turned from him and trailed after Brenda as the actress worked her way out of the room, which was not an easy progress, as so many people still wanted a memorable moment with her.

Brenda went to sleep immediately upon her head hitting the pillow when they'd gotten back to their room. But Charlotte tossed and turned for a while, working what was appearing to be too many coincidences over in her mind. And when she did get to sleep, it was only to dream a sequence of coincidences, all of which ended with her waking to the thought that there were no coincidence in life—that she didn't believe in them.

Eventually she did sleep, only to be awakened near dawn by the sound of a familiar noise. It took her a few minutes of coming up out of a deep, troubled sleep to recognize the sound. It was the sound of a powerful engine out on the water. The same sound she'd heard in Hopewell. The engines of a cigarette boat. And now that she thought about it, she was aware that there had been at least three cigarette speedboats tied up to the plantation's pier when they had arrived earlier that afternoon.

What in the hell did Pattie Parker's operation need with three cigarette speedboats, a fully awake Charlotte wondered. With the identical sound to that of the drug operation boat on the Choptank River at night in Maryland.

Yet another coincidence for Charlotte to doubt. She got very little sleep for the rest of the night.

Chapter Eight: One Dead Chinaman

Brenda stirred in the bed as the sounds of the motorboat engines died into the distance. Rolling onto her back, she turned toward Charlotte, who already was dressed and sitting across the room. Still sleepy eyed, the actress stretched and yawned, once again giving Charlotte the thought that she certainly wished she would look that good coming out of sleep. She wished she looked that good dressed for a ball.

"I was disoriented there for a moment," Brenda murmured. "I thought I was waking up at the cottage in

Hopewell. Wishful thinking, I suppose. I was wondering why the dogs weren't after us to get up and feed them."

"It probably was the sound of the motorboat engines. You heard the sounds coming from the Choptank when we were back in Hopewell."

"Motorboat engines?"

"Yes, the same sound came from out on the water here. I remember having seen three of those cigarette boats, like the one that was running drugs into the swamp in Hopewell, tied up to the pier here."

"My goodness, what time is it?" Brenda asked, as she rolled over to the side of the bed and sat up.

"Just past 6:00 a.m. Why don't you get up and get dressed, Brenda? I think it's past time that we moved into the city. Gordon said we'd be welcome at the college president's house, which is in the thick of the Spoleto performance venues."

"My god, Charlotte, what are you doing?" Brenda only now focused on Charlotte, sitting across the room, in the gloom of the dawn hour.

"I'm cleaning my handgun."

"Whatever for?"

"I told you I don't like coincidences—don't believe in them. There have been too many going on around here. I do believe in premonitions. And I had dreams of my own last night. I think Pattie Parker means to harm you for some reason and that . . . well, that there are too many apparent coincidences going on around here. I've packed our bags—although I'm sure you'll have heart palpitations when you see how I've just thrown everything in. But it's a good thing you're awake. It's time we clear out of here . . . before the household is awake."

She stood and pulled on a light jacket that covered the slight bulge of the gun holster under her armpit. The jacket also covered the badge hooked at her waist to her belt. She had been deputized the previous day at the Charleston FBI office.

Brenda bounded out of the bed and headed for the en suite bathroom without further question, and the two were poised at the top of the stairs, luggage in hand, within twenty minutes.

Charlotte had miscalculated the part about getting up before the household was awake. At the top of the stairs, she drew back and lifted a finger to her lips. Peeking over the landing railing, they could see that Cameron Reed was below, decked out in camouflage gear. They moved down the stairs silently after they saw him stride out of the house and down the front steps. He was moving toward the pier, where one of the cigarette boats just now was returning. There was a solitary figure in the boat, but whoever it was couldn't be identified from the house. Reed's yellow float plane was floating out in the sea beyond.

"I wonder where he's going," Brenda whispered, as they moved around the front of the house to the parking apron at the side.

"Chances are very good that he's flying south for another load of drugs," Charlotte said. "To be packaged here and distributed by motorboat at night all along the coast. Just like the operation in Hopewell."

"Like the drugs at Curtain Call?" Brenda asked, aghast.

"I think maybe exactly like the operation at Curtain Call. This is what I meant about too many coincidences, Brenda. I think we've left the unraveling of a major drug operation, only to land dead center in another part of the same operation. I didn't tell you yesterday, because I didn't want to alarm you, but I found plastic packets just like the ones containing drugs in Madge Miller's room, in the packaging building here. This may be where they cut the drugs and package them when they bring them into the States.

"And, if Pattie Parker is behind any of this," she continued, "I think this is a very dangerous place for us to be— that she means for you to be here. So, the best thing we can do for the moment is not be here."

As Brenda drove toward Charleston, Charlotte remembered that she was supposed to be in cell phone contact with Evan first thing this morning. She was beginning to think she understood why he had come down to Charleston and that it wasn't primarily to wine and dine Shirley Elgin. The thought of that lifted her spirits even while she recognized that it shouldn't affect them at all.

Checking her own phone, she saw that she'd had it switched off. So, if Evan had tried to call her, he hadn't been able to get through. As soon as she turned the phone on, it rang.

"Evan?" she asked instinctively as she put the phone to her ear.

"No, it's Shirley Elgin." The voice sounded a bit cold—but Charlotte understood why it should.

"Yes, Shirley. Sorry, Evan said he had to talk to me about something this morning, but we haven't caught up with each other yet."

"Evan's at my office. He won't be available for a while, I don't think. We picked up that couple you told the Baltimore police about—and I do wish you had told me as well—Clagett and Nusbaum. That couple you reported as being part of a drug operation up in Maryland where you live. Evan knew all about the case, so I left him at the office to interview them. It may fit something we're working."

"You say you left him at the office? Is that where you want me to go? I can do so after I leave Brenda off at Simons Center. She's practicing with the jazz ensemble backing her up at the festival."

"No. Go ahead and park at the president's house or the Simons Center garage. I'm right across the street from there—at the Cistern Yard. Come here. I didn't call you because of the couple we picked up."

"The Cistern Yard. What do you need with me there?"

Charlotte immediately regretted wording it that way. She fully realized that Shirley didn't feel she needed Charlotte anywhere. The pause before Elgin answered confirmed that this was the way she felt about it.

"I'm calling you in because Evan asked me to—because FBI headquarters has cleared you for consulting on the potential Chinese espionage case at Spoleto. There's one dead Chinaman here and two members of the troupe have flown away. This is either part of a plan we were worried about or a real mess. The director of Spoleto said you were talking with the victim and other members of the troupe. You may have some idea what gives. But, anyway, Evan asked me to inform you and bring you into this. So that's what I'm doing. He also asked me to tell you to clear out of the tea plantation where you're staying."

"We've already done that. I'll be there at the Cistern Yard faster than you'll expect." When she clicked off, she didn't say why it would be faster than expected. It would be fast because Brenda was at the wheel of the Jag, her oversized sunglasses in place, a scarf streaming in the wind behind her, doing her Grace Kelly thing.

For once Brenda couldn't be driving fast enough for Charlotte's mood.

* * * *

After leaving Brenda off at the Simons Center, greeting and giving hugs all around with the jazz musicians who would be backing up her performance, which was a bit of a chore because Brenda kept saying she could stick with Charlotte if she needed the support, Charlotte drove the Jaguar down the street to the college president's house. Here the house stewards, apprised that the women were moving in, directed her to park under a carport next to the garages and picked up their luggage. From there it was a short walk to the Cistern Yard.

As she approached the small park by that name in the center of the college, Charlotte had the image of a small circus either setting up or breaking down. There were uniformed policemen marking off the area with yellow tape and, because she had been FBI, she was able to pick out several FBI agents as well. As was natural, the two separate law enforcement groups were squared off against each other as if there had been a turf battle out here, which she thought there probably had been. If it was a suspicious death case, as Shirley Elgin had indicated to her on the phone, the city police would assume they had jurisdiction. But if it was one of the Chinese citizen acrobats there for the festival, a troupe the FBI already was scrutinizing, who had been killed, the FBI certainly would assert its primacy.

In addition to them, there was an assortment of festival performers who had happened upon the crime scene in their midst. Prominent among them were the Chinese acrobats themselves. The one person Charlotte expected to see but didn't was Shirley Elgin. There, though, was another senior FBI agent who she'd met at the FBI office the previous day and who was talking with a policemen and Gordon Galworthy. Galworthy saw Charlotte and called to her, which caused the FBI agent to look in her direction too. He motioned for Charlotte to come under the tape and over to where he stood.

As Charlotte walked toward them, she let her eyes scan those standing around who looked like they were part of the Chinese acrobat troupe. She didn't see any of the performers she'd talked with the previous night: Li Fen, Huang Bao, or Feng Da. The young man who hadn't said anything but seemed to understand English and the Wardrobe mistress were there, though. The other acrobats around seemed to be standing close to this woman and watching her for direction.

"My god, Charlotte, they think it might have been murder—by one or two of the Chinese acrobats, and the FBI has swooped right in," Gordon said as she came close. "I don't understand."

"There's an issue with the acrobatic troupe, Gordon," Charlotte said. "They were just being watched. I knew about it but wasn't able to tell you anything." Before Galworthy could say anything else, though, she turned to the FBI agent, who obviously remembered her from the previous day. "Agent Elgin called me to come over. Is she here?"

"She was called away to another operation," the agent said, "but she told me you were coming and that I should fill you in on everything. She said you had talked to the victim last night."

Oh, no, Charlotte thought. Which of the three is it?

"What, yet another FBI agent showing up to tromp all over our murder scene?" The outburst had come from the police officer talking to the FBI agent and Galworthy.

"Please, officer," the agent said. "This is a national security matter. This would have come to us anyway."

"This is a murder in my city," the policeman said.

"Please, gentlemen," Charlotte interjected, holding up a hand toward each of the belligerent sides. "Agent, if you could just give me the short version on this, I'll see what I can find out from the other acrobats. Who is the victim?"

The agent consulted an e-tablet he was carrying. He raised a palm toward the police officer to cut him off long enough to brief Charlotte and, lo and behold, it worked. "The victim is Feng Da, who was the leader of the troupe, I take it. Two of the acrobats are missing, a male, named Huang Bao, and a female by the name of Li Fen. This may have been the breakaway we anticipated, but maybe the troupe leader wasn't in on it, there was a dust up, and he got his head bashed in."

"That's possible," Charlotte said, hoping it wasn't, because she had liked both Li Fen and Huang Bao. "I ascertained last night that Feng Da was the security officer in the troupe—they apparently always have them when Chinese groups travel abroad—as much to keep tabs on the group members as to protect them. If it's OK, I'll go on over to talk with the acrobats over there to see if I can shed any more light on what happened."

She left the FBI agent and police officer to argue jurisdiction, and Gordon Galworthy to be confused and worried, and went, first, to where the body was lying. He was crumpled at the base of a stone wall, of seating height, that wound around in the small park area. She could tell just by looking over the shoulder of the medical examiner that he had died of a head wound. There was a smear of blood on the top of the wall above where he lay. It didn't take a genius to figure out that he'd hit his head on that—or that his head had been pounded on the top of the wall. There was no reason to believe that he'd been murdered rather than just slipped and fell against the stone wall other than the evidence in the sand of the walkway. That showed much more scuffing there than anywhere else on the path. That and the fact that two of the acrobats in his troupe had been reported missing.

She then walked over to the milling group of Chinese acrobats. She walked straight up to the wardrobe mistress, but then she turned her head to the young man who had listened but not spoken the previous night.

"Am I right in thinking that you speak and understand English well?"

"Well enough," he answered. He had the cultured diction of an Englishman, so Charlotte knew that he spoke it quite well enough for her purposes.

"Could you translate for me then, please? I want to ask the wardrobe mistress a few questions. I hope to be able to help. She's the true leader of this troupe, I gather?"

The young man nodded his head in confirmation and then turned and spoke to the wardrobe mistress, who gave a guarded little smile and also nodded her head to Charlotte.

"Ask her, please, if she thinks that either Huang Bao or Li Fen could have done this maliciously. And whether she thinks they are trying to defect."

An exchange ensued and the young man answered. "Comrade Tian says that only time will tell on what Bao or Fen might have done. But she does not think either one would desert their country. She just thinks they are frightened and perhaps are lost somewhere in the city."

"Could you ask her—"

"I think Comrade Tian would like to help you further but cannot do so. Perhaps you are asking the wrong person. Bao and Fen are good friends of mine."

"So, can you tell me anything of use?" Charlotte asked as she turned her full attention to the young man. "I only met them last night, but I feel that they are my friends too. I would like to help them, if possible."

"Whatever happened to Feng Da last night, it was not on purpose—beyond his own purpose."

"Please tell me what you know, what, if anything you saw."

"After we talked with you at the banquet last night, Li Fen said she would like to see this park you told her about at the tip of the city. Feng Da said that no seeing of the area outside of where we practice and perform was permitted—that it wasn't on the schedule. But then later, I heard him tell Li Fen that he would show her the park if she liked—right then, in the dark of last night. She left with him . . . and I saw Huang Bao follow."

"Do you have reason to believe that Feng Da would harm Li Fen in any way?"

There was a pause before the young man said, "Bao and Fen are very close. Bao seemed very worried when he left after they did."

Charlotte decided she'd heard enough to be able to figure out what happened here, and she also had an idea where to find the frightened couple—and thought they had good reason to be frightened.

She went back to the FBI agent and the police officer, who were still arguing. Gordon Galworthy had left.

"I've talked with the Chinese," she said, "And I don't think we have a federal case here, Agent. I suggest that we let the city police take the lead for now—and that we should not be too quick to consider this a premeditated murder. I think I know where the missing acrobats can be found and that I can bring them here. But perhaps you both could thin out your ranks so that they aren't spooked if I can bring them back. I don't think we have a case that will require a show of force."

"You need anyone to go with you?" The question came from a mollified police officer.

"I don't think so. I think I can best do this alone."

It was a nine-block walk down to Battery Park from the college campus, and Charlotte had to stop to catch her breath as she got to the edge of the park. But by then she had seen them, sitting on a bench facing Charleston Harbor and away from her line of approach.

She walked to them slowly and sat down on the bench beside them. Li Fen had what was probably the dinner jacket Huang Bao had been wearing the previous night draped around her shoulders, and the two were huddled close together. Both had obviously been crying.

"Am I right that you're wearing the jacket because your dress is torn?" she asked in a gentle voice. It was clear that they had recognized her when she sat down on the bench. It also was a warm day. The jacket wasn't necessary to stave off the cold. Li Fen was trembling for another reason, Charlotte knew.

Li Fen just nodded and snuffled.

"It was an accident, wasn't it? Huang Bao just came to your aid there in the park, and Feng Da fell and hit his head against the stone wall in the scuffle."

127

Li Fen nodded again.

"I know your first instinct was to run away. That is understandable. But I've talked with the wardrobe mistress. I think she understands—everything. And she said she knows you weren't running away to leave China and live in America. I think if you come back with me now, all will be explained and everything will be all right. You'll come back with me now, won't you?"

Both of the young people nodded their heads.

"I'm tired of walking, though, so why don't I ask if one of those horse-drawn carriages over there can take us back. Wouldn't that be something special you could tell all of your friends that you did while you were in Charleston?"

She received a hint of a smile from both of them then. And, since she had a greater job to do, she threw in the next two questions just to confirm her suspicions. "Neither of you are nuclear scientists, are you?"

They swiveled their heads toward her at that point and gave her a surprised and confused look. There was truth in those expressions. Charlotte was an expert in assessing reactions to surprise questions.

"And no one else in the troupe is a nuclear scientist either, are they?"

Surprise and confusion remained on the faces.

"No, I didn't think so." This Charlotte murmured to herself.

After she'd gotten the pair back to the Cistern Yard, and the wardrobe mistress had been brought forth to help verify the nature of the victim and the basic truth of what had happened in the Cistern Yard the previous evening, Charlotte decided to check in with Brenda's rehearsal.

As she started to walk away, though, the FBI agent in charge at the scene hailed her. "There's a phone call here for you, Agent Diamond."

It was Shirley Elgin again. "Evan has insisted you would want to be on this operation and that he wants you here, so I suggest you come out—"

"What operation? Come out where, Agent Elgin?"

"The tea plantation. Agent Worthington insisted that you will want to be in on this. I'm leaving orders at the gate to let you through. But park where they show you and come in quietly on foot. And you'll want to hurry or you'll miss the fun."

"Is Evan there? Can you put him on the phone?" But the line had already been cut.

Charlotte wasted no time getting back to the Jaguar parked at the president's home and roaring out of town toward the tea plantation. She was grateful Brenda wasn't there, or she never again could rag on Brenda about driving too fast.

Chapter Nine: Reading the Tea Leaves

Charlotte brought the Jag to a hard stop on the dirt road leading into the tea plantation in a spray of pebbles and flurry of dust that had the bullet-proof-vested FBI agent posted at the gate covering his eyes and nose and retreating for cover. He'd clearly been told to let the distinctive roadster through, though, and directed her to park on a grassy patch just inside the gate where there were several other black SUVs—all FBI vehicles, Charlotte assumed. They had government tags.

"Is Agent Evans from the Annapolis office here?" she asked the agent who came around to open her door.

"I don't know, ma'am, but an operation is under way down the road. You'll need to proceed on foot from here—and quietly. But you'd need to be badged and—"

As she got out of the convertible, Charlotte held her jacket open to display both the badge and that she was armed.

The agent looked surprised, as if he wouldn't have guessed that a woman looking like her would also be an FBI agent. "Here, ma'am," he said, as he started to unbutton his vest, "You'd better take this too. There might be some action up there."

"I couldn't take your vest. You'll need—"

"There are others in the vehicles here. Let me help you get this on." He proceeded to do so, Charlotte having a bit of a problem getting it closed over her chest. She had taken off her jacket and she restrapped the gun holster over the vest and cradled the handgun in her hand.

The agent stood back from her, and Charlotte just knew that he was working hard to suppress a grin. "You just follow this road, ma'am, and—"

"I know the way," Charlotte said. "I've been here before."

She trotted off, leaving the agent to scratch his head at the incongruity of such a large, middle-aged woman being so calm and in control in the face of an FBI operation.

Charlotte moved as quickly as her bulk and conditioning permitted, crouching down and holding the gun in front of her, proceeding as quietly as she could on the side of the road and using the brush there as cover. She came upon an agent crouched behind a tree within sight of the plantation outbuildings and surveilling the area in that direction. She knew that he would be part of a perimeter setup.

He motioned her to stop, and she crept up beside him and showed him the badge pinned to her waist. "Shirley Elgin called me in," she whispered. "Evan Worthington. The senior agent at the Annapolis office. Have you seen him here?"

The agent shrugged.

"What's going on here?" Charlotte whispered. "Agent Elgin didn't say. She just said I'd want to be in on it."

"A major drug operation bust," he answered. "We've been working on it for months and just got the tipoff that drugs were coming in."

"I knew it. No such thing as coincidences," she muttered.

The agent gave her a quizzical look, but he didn't try to stop Charlotte as she moved on, toward the twin packaging buildings she had been shown earlier when she'd been given the tour. Her interest was the second building—the one the plantation worker Jose Almirez had avoided showing her. She had little doubt now what that building was really used for. The drugs would be brought into the States in bulk. They had to be cut and packaged somewhere.

As she came closer to the buildings, the door on the suspect one opened and a man appeared in the doorway. He was in the shadows still, but he was holding what looked like a handgun. He wasn't wearing an FBI vest. A chill went through Charlotte's body when she realized that it was Jose Almirez. She hit the deck, hoping that he hadn't seen her. Apparently he hadn't, as he drew back into the building as another man came up behind him. Almirez turned at that, his gun drawn, and the two men disappeared into the shadows of the building's interior. The other man was Evan Worthington.

Evan was in the building. And Jose Almirez was there too. Had Evan stumbled onto the drug packaging building and been caught by Almirez? The various thoughts of what was happening ran through Charlotte's mind. She looked out across the tea fields toward the plantation house and the ocean beyond. She could see the backs of FBI agents fanned out behind cover in the tea fields and on the house's lawn. They were all pointed toward the oceanfront. The fringe of palmetto trees at the edge of the water kept Charlotte from being able to see beyond that point. But she knew that the action the agents were focused on was in the other direction, not here. And they were too far away for her to hail without alerting Jose Almirez to her presence.

They also were too far away for her to go to them and muster them to come back with her to aid Evan. There simply would not be time. And whatever they were creeping up on may be more important to them than Evan was to them. Most likely it was. She and Evan were just seen as interlopers in a long-developing operation. This was one time that Charlotte was glad that Shirley Elgin had a crush on Evan; she'd do what she could to save him . . . if she were here. But she wasn't here.

Whatever the agents out there were doing wasn't as important to Charlotte as Evan was.

Jose couldn't fire a shot without drawing attention from the agents over toward the oceanfront. But who knows what else he might have at hand to quietly dispatch Evan?

Without another thought, Charlotte crept closer to the packaging buildings until she was there, beside the one she'd been given a tour of. She crept along the wall of that and around the corner. When she was against the wall of the targeted building without having been detected, she gulped in air, trying to steady her grip on the handgun she held in front of her in two hands.

Instinctively remembering her training, she turned and burst through the door, keeping low, and jagging and rolling on the floor to one side to take advantage of the element of surprise and to be less of a target.

The two men standing at the back of the room, which was crammed with drugs in various stages of being cut, measured, and packaged, looked up in surprise.

A voice rang out, "No, Charlotte, don't."

But the cry came too late to arrest her action.

* * * *

Charlotte gave a nervous laugh, lowered her gun, and let out a groan from the instinctive maneuver she had accomplished, but not without pain. The first thing she had seen as she rolled into the room onto the floor and facing the back of the building was the flash of light on the badge hooked to Jose Almirez' belt.

He was an FBI agent too. And what he was holding in his hand only sort of resembled a handgun. It was a camera. The two of them had been cataloging evidence of the drug operation in the building.

Evan and Jose were laughing too, but it was a very nervous laugh.

"When the two of you are finished being amused, could one of you come over and help me up," Charlotte muttered. "With luck I haven't broken anything."

Evan did the honors, giving Charlotte an extra hug that wasn't necessary in the crane lift operation. "You were coming to save me, were you?"

"You seemed to need saving at the time," she said somewhat huffily, embarrassed that she was hugging him back, clearly showing not only her relief but also her affection.

Turning to Jose then, she said, "So you were working here undercover?"

"Yes, ma'am."

"And you didn't have to check for me where the plastic bags with the green palm tree embossed on them were ordered from, did you? You already knew the same packets were used to package tea and drugs."

"Yes, ma'am."

"And you didn't reveal that to me, even having heard I was a retired agent."

"Yes, ma'am. Sorry, ma'am."

"Don't be sorry. You did exactly right—even though it came close to getting your head blown off. I certainly would have regretted having done that. But you were holding cover well. I'll remember to mention that to Shirley Elgin. I assume you're one of her agents."

"Yes, ma'am, I am." He was beaming at the praise. He had heard of Charlotte's reputation.

"You're one lucky man that Charlotte Diamond's instincts are sharp as a tack," Worthington interjected. "I told you you should have put on an FBI vest."

"But Agent Elgin told me not to—in case I still needed to maintain my cover."

"I guess I wish my agents followed my orders so doggedly," Evan conceded. "I think we can leave Jose to the work here," he turned to say to Charlotte. "The others are catching the drug delivery in progress—or I hope they are. I know you'll want to be in on that. Shall we?" He ushered Charlotte out of the building, with her going along willingly. She just hoped to hell that it wasn't just Cameron Reed involved. She so wanted for this to be pinned on Pattie Parker as well.

Outside of the building, Evan came to a halt. "Are you OK, Charlotte? You took quite a fall in rolling into the building. I didn't want to say anything in front of Jose. Did you hurt anything?"

"Only my pride," she answered. In fact she hurt all over, but she wasn't able to tell Evan that. "If ever I needed a reminder that I've gotten too old for field work, that was the wakeup call."

"You're doing just fine on field work. But you could stay and watch from here," Evan said. "There's a pair of binoculars back in the—"

"Not on your life, buster," Charlotte growled. "This is something I want to see with my own eyes—up close and very, very personal."

When they caught up with the cordon of FBI agents, taking their time in crouching low and moving from cover to cover, a maneuver that made Charlotte's aching body scream, happily in silence, the agents were fanned out along the rise from the narrow beach where the line of palmetto palms shielded them from the ocean. That they were mostly palmetto trees they were hiding behind made Charlotte chuckle given the circumstances of the case. Evan and Charlotte moved to a position beside Shirley Elgin, who was lying prone, facing the ocean, and looking out to sea through binoculars.

Evan went down on his belly beside her and Charlotte did what she could, with a distinct groan, to do the same on the other side of him.

"What's coming down?" Evan whispered to Elgin. Charlotte scanned the beach and pier area, looking for some reason why they'd be whispering, but she saw no one nearby other than FBI agents with clearly marked vests on. She wrote the whispering off to the drama of the situation and kept her voice low as well.

"We're waiting for them to start transferring the drugs. Then we'll have them red-handed," Elgin responded.

Charlotte could see that down the line from either side of her FBI agents were filming out to sea with cameras sporting humongous telescopic lenses. "What are we looking for?" She asked. "I can't see anything out there."

"Can you see that red dot out there? That's a float plane. It's just landed near the fishing boat beside it. The fishing boat left from this pier as we were making our approach. The house is deserted, so we're assuming Pattie Parker is on the fishing boat. And Cameron Reed must have picked up the drugs somewhere farther south and flown them up here. The whole operation appears to be a relay up the East Coast from South America."

"And Regina Quinn too?" Charlotte asked. "I was told that Quinn owns and operates the fishing boat."

"Yes, maybe. Or maybe just Quinn."

"I certainly hope Parker is in on this too," Charlotte said. Then her memory was jogged and she blurted out, "Red? Did you say the plane was red?"

"Yes."

"The plane I saw Reed with—the one he flew out of here this morning—was yellow. And how far south could he have gotten and then back here from about 7:00 a.m. this morning? That's when I saw him last—leaving the plantation house, wearing camouflage."

"We'll have to ask him that when we nab him," Elgin muttered. "And maybe he just exchanged planes down south to save the refueling time."

Charlotte was about to speak again when an excited voice was raised from one of the cameramen. "Go, go, go," he cried out, waving his hands. "Two figures are starting to transfer something from the plane's hold into the rowboat they've taken from the fishing boat. There's someone in the cockpit still, so there are three of them at least."

"Yes, now!" Shirley Elgin cried out as she raised up on her feet and, along with the line of FBI agents, raced toward the pier. Charlotte and Evan lagged behind, because Evan had to help a complaining Charlotte get vertical again.

They took the three cigarette motorboats tied up to the pier, overloading each. Evan and Charlotte barely caught the third one. Shirley Elgin was in the first.

It was a race to the plane and fishing boat in order to get close enough to head off evasive action before those transferring the drugs or the floatplane pilot could react.

The cigarette boats were swift even loaded to the gunwales as they were, and two of them went into swimming circles around the plane and rowboat to keep them from moving while the boat Elgin was in pulled up to the rowboat and swarmed over the two figures who were unloading the plane. The fishing boat, off to the side a good hundred feet, remained stationary, without any evidence of anyone aboard, so everyone was assuming no one was on the boat—which subsequently proved to be correct.

Charlotte was close enough to the action to see that it was Pattie Parker and Regina Quinn who were in the rowboat. Each had several wrapped articles in their hands shaped like bricks. The cameramen were clicking and recording away with both still and video cameras.

"Got you," Charlotte called out, in a triumphant voice. Pattie Parker turned a sour, hateful expression in her direction. Charlotte dearly hoped that Pattie recognized her voice.

But then she looked over to the floatplane. The motorboat she was in had circled around to the cockpit of the plane and was both close enough and far enough away for

Charlotte to clearly see through the windscreen who was sitting at the controls.

"That's not Cameron Reed," she sang out, grabbing Evan's sleeve to redirect his attention.

"It's not?"

"No. That's Wendell Miller."

"Wendell who?"

"Wendell Miller. The son of Madge Miller, murdered at Curtain Call, with a connection to this drug operation. And brother of Walt Miller, also murdered that night. It's Wendell Miller, Evan. I should have figured it out already. He told us he operated a charter plane service from out of the Florida Keys. That's the connection between here and the South American suppliers. He's the one flying the drugs up the East Coast."

Chapter Ten: There Are No Coincidences

A blue indigo mood was in full swing the next evening as, under a full moon in a clear star-lit sky, punctuated with the twinkling of fireflies, Brenda Brandon came out onto the small wooden stage set before the folding chairs of an applauding overflow crowd in the Cistern Yard. Under blue-tinted spotlights, with the backing of the Joey Bent Jazz Quartet, and a renewed smattering of applause, she opened in a low, husky voice with "When the deep purple falls over sleepy garden walls, and the stars begin to flicker in the night . . ."

So many people had come to hear Brenda that the chairs that had been set out on the lawn didn't accommodate them. People were sitting along the stone wall that wound through the little park and bordered it from the streets on two sides. More people were standing on the sidewalks bordering two sides of the park. The only available space was where Feng Da had died in the early hours of the previous day. The spot had been cleaned up, but concert attendees avoided it as if instinctively knowing that some tragedy had unfolded there, even if it was of Feng Da's own doing.

Brenda's own contingent of personal supporters was large. In addition to Charlotte and Gordon Galworthy, Evan Worthington and Shirley Elgin were there—as was a surprise addition. Aaron Woolridge, the producer of most of the films Brenda had acted in with David Runyon had flown in that morning from Hollywood especially to attend Brenda's opening-night performance at the Spoleto Festival. He had surprised Brenda by walking in on her rehearsal that afternoon.

"Aaron, you came," Brenda had said, clearly pleased.

"I wouldn't miss it for the world, sugar." Woolridge had answered. "One of the dumbest opportunities we missed in doing your movies was not putting more clips of you singing in them."

Brenda arranged with the jazz musicians backing her performance to have supper with them after a succeeding performance. Although the college president was away for a conference, Gordon Galworthy had arranged a small, private buffet for Brenda and her contingent at the nearby president's house that evening so that Brenda wouldn't be mobbed in a more public venue.

As they sat around the parlor drinking coffee after the meal, and the platitudes for Brenda's spectacular performance were beginning to be circular, the conversation turned to the events of recent days.

"What made you move on the drug operation at the tea plantation when you did?" Charlotte asked, turning to Shirley Elgin. Shirley was sitting very close to Evan, just as Charlotte was snuggling up to Brenda. Charlotte found that she didn't care, and it was comforting to see that Brenda was reciprocating in the cuddling far more than Evan was.

The natural concern for Evan's welfare the previous day had come with a revelation. She did love the big lug, but not in the way she loved Brenda. She loved him as a best friend. And she wanted him to be happy—and she wanted all thoughts that she and he could be a pair to fade away. If he was happy with Shirley Elgin—which Shirley seemed to be exhibiting more than he was—than that was OK with Charlotte. She had hers in the form of Brenda, and that was more than enough for her. Charlotte didn't dislike Shirley and assumed she'd be more friendly and less threatened the more she realized that Charlotte was no competition for her in the Evan department. Of course it would help if Evan cooperated in showing that, as well.

"That couple you led us to—Kurt Clagett and Annie Nusbaum," Shirley said. "They sang like birds for Evan once he suggested that they weren't just wanted for drug dealing but also for murder. They were quick to give up Pattie Parker and the tea plantation as the center of a massive drug operation all along the lower East Coast. The two had some insight into how the drugs were moved and when we could expect a shipment to come to the tea plantation. My office had been watching the tea plantation for months, just looking for enough evidence to move. We wanted to catch a shipment coming in. Those drugs packaged in the packets with the palm tree embossed on them had begun to appear at this college—and also down at the Savannah College of Art and Design. Clagett and Nusbaum admitted to pushing drugs on both of those campuses."

Charlotte let it pass that Elgin had an operation going that she knew Charlotte was interested in and hadn't told her anything about it before now. She was in too mellow of a mood this evening to fight. Still, if Elgin had been forthcoming, everything probably could have been cleaned up quicker.

"Poor Evonne," Brenda said. "She'll be so upset her husband's nephew was involved and that she hired Anne Nusbaum. But what about Wendell Miller?"

"Well, we now know he was involved up to his neck— partners at the top with Pattie Parker and Regina Quinn," Worthington answered. "But Clagett and Nusbaum held that back. Or they didn't get around to it in that first interview. And just maybe they didn't know where he fit in the hierarchy. After the incident at Curtain Call, they surely knew he was involved in some way.

"They said a shipment was due in yesterday, so I immediately went off to alert Shirley to the opportunity to intercept that. I had told them they were suspected of murder, but I didn't get around to questioning them about that then. When I came back later in the day, after we'd already apprehended Miller, the two of them wanted to make perfectly clear that it was Miller—not either of them—who had killed his mother and brother. Clagett said he wasn't even there when the Millers were killed. The drug delivery was late and he had a buy to get to at Johns Hopkins, so he took some of the stash Madge Miller had in her room and took off for Baltimore. Wendell's the one who told Clagett to go ahead and return to Baltimore early that evening to do his drug deal there. Miller told Clagett—according to Clagett—that he would meet the delivery from the cigarette boat in the swamp by Curtain Call that night The nurse, Anne Nusbaum backed up that story in a separate interview. She said Clagett was gone before Madge Miller was killed—and that she went into the room and found the woman dead after Wendell Miller had left.

"Madge died because she got religion and not only was going to stop pushing the drugs, but she also was going to turn herself in. Walt Miller died because Madge had told him what she was doing. Apparently she didn't tell him that his own brother was her supplier. But Wendell Miller couldn't be sure she hadn't, so he killed his brother when he had the chance."

"And we thought that Cameron Reed was the one flying the drugs in," Charlotte said. "But his only sin was going along with Pattie about being married to him, doing some machinery maintenance for her, and fooling around with her when she wanted him to. As we first surmised, it was Pattie and Regina Quinn who were the real couple. Cameron had only been brought in—either to please Pattie for some reason or because he was paid to pose as her husband—simply because he resembled Brenda's old friend and perpetual leading man, David Runyon. Pattie just wanted to torment Brenda."

"But that's the part I don't understand," Brenda said. "Not just that Pattie seemed to have it in for me, but also that she went out of her way to involve Curtain Call in her drug route."

"Oh, I think I can answer that," Aaron Woolridge piped up. "I just got here and only today heard what was going on, but it's part of the reason I came to the festival. I wanted to warn Brenda off of Pattie. After Pattie had tried to implicate Brenda in the death of Helga Lund, the movie studio producers—me at the forefront—got together and blackballed Pattie for movie roles. We already knew she was poison, but when she would stoop to do that to one of our major box-office actresses . . ."

He didn't complete the sentence, but Charlotte completed the idea for him. "And Pattie Parker blamed Brenda for her blackballing rather than the movie studios."

"Apparently so," Woolridge responded. "When she left Hollywood, it was rumored that she declared she'd ruin Brenda if it was the last thing she did. I and other producers were aghast that it took this turn, but we were more determined than ever not to offer her another movie part."

"And she knew that Curtain Call was everything to me, so that's where she attacked me," Brenda said. Her voice was contemplative, as if she never could have thought there could be such evil in a person.

And Charlotte loved her for that at that moment as never before.

"But that night . . . the night Madge Miller and Walt died, Wendell Miller left Hopewell. But then he came back," Brenda said.

"He probably got down the road, cooled off from having just zeroed out his family, and realized that leaving as he did made him an obvious suspect," Charlotte said. "So, he came back, admitted to having fought with his mother over being a drug pusher, and did a clever job of rising above suspicion. And we all bought that hook, line, and sinker. I sure am getting rusty at the detection work. I could have focused on Wendell then. One of the residents told me that Madge was giving the drug operation up—that she'd found religion. I could have gotten corroboration on that from other residents. Wendell told us in his first interview that he was in Hopewell because Walt told him their mother wouldn't give up the drug dealing. When I was a working agent, I would have honed in on that discrepancy immediately. I should just give it up."

"Not in my book," Evan said hotly. "Nobody could say that who had seen you roll into that building at the tea plantation, perfectly set to blow some perpetrator's head off/ They wouldn't say that if they saw the Charlotte in action I saw."

Everyone laughed at that, although Shirley Elgin only did so perfunctorily. Until she'd safely landed Evan Worthington, she'd never be likely to stop seeing Charlotte as competition.

"Such a coincidence, though," Gordon Galworthy spoke for the first time. "A drug operation both here and up in Maryland, and Brenda and Charlotte both here and up in Maryland. Brenda being invited to perform at Spoleto."

"That was no coincidence," Charlotte said, with a snort. "There are no coincidences—certainly not in this. It all revolved around Pattie and her plans to bring Brenda down. She's the one who chose Curtain Call as an extension of her drug pushing business. And you yourself, Gordon, said that she first put the bug in your ear to have Brenda down here to perform. We weren't here by coincidence. Pattie planned it all."

"And the Chinese acrobatic troupe. Your being asked to look to that, Charlotte?" Gordon wasn't giving up completely on the coincidence idea.

"That was separate, and Evan didn't ask me to look into that until we already were coming to Charleston and the Spoleto Festival."

"I worry about that poor young Chinese couple," Brenda said. "What will happen to them over the death of that man?"

"I think the true leader of the troupe, the wardrobe mistress, has done much to help those two young people," Charlotte said. "She acknowledged that she had her eye on Feng Da for showing too much interest in the young women in the troupe. She'd already reported on him back to Beijing, which will help establish that he was up to no good with Li Fen. And she supported Li Fen's and Huang Bao's story that it had not been anything more than to prevent Feng Da's assault on Li Fen. I'm sure her judgment will go a long way in convincing the Chinese government that it was an accident of Feng Da's making. Now, for the American authorities . . ."

"I think we've worked that out," Shirley Elgin spoke up to say. "Neither of our governments wants to make more out of it than what it probably was. Just Feng Da's own fault—and an accident during a fall in a fight he was fully engaged in."

"The acrobats, including Li Fen and Huang Bao, have been cleared to perform as scheduled," Galworthy confirmed. "And there doesn't seem to be any continuing media coverage on the death."

"I don't think you need have fears of the intent of any of the acrobats—or of the Chinese government in using the acrobats, either," Charlotte said, looking at both Evan and Shirley. "I talked with them enough to be convinced they are only what they purport to be—acrobats, who might like to do a turn in Las Vegas, but who are only acrobats and have no intention of leaving China permanently. Acrobats are like rock stars in China, is my impression—much more than they would be here. And from what I could get out of the wardrobe woman, I wouldn't be surprised if the Chinese government itself didn't float the rumors you heard about the troupe members' intentions just so that the FBI *would* watch them closely and make sure they went home."

Evan was quick to agree. Shirley wasn't so quick, but she did seem interested in following Evan's lead, so she just nodded her head.

Charlotte got the feeling—happily—that the Chinese acrobat troupe case was closed.

It was late and others were yawning—Brenda looked like she was about to wilt, if Brenda was ever capable of looking like she was about to wilt—so, to help bring the evening to a close, she lifted her coffee cup, and said, "By way of proposing a goodnight, I lift my glass in a toast." The others lifted their cups as well. "To palm trees."

"Meaning?" Aaron Woolridge asked.

"It was a green palm tree, embossed on little plastic packets, that was the glue in merging the elements of our dear departed mystery. In the end we just followed the palm. So, I lift my glass to—"

"Following the palm tree," all said in unison, with laughter all around, as they all stood, tired, but happy—and ultimately satisfied with the unfolding of life about them.

~

(A sneak peek at Olivia Stowe's next book)

Final Flight

A Blue Ridge Mystery

by

Olivia Stowe

Chapter One of *Final Flight*:
"Fire on the Mountain"

"Come away from the window, Clara. Come back to bed. We don't have long."

"Did you see that, Stan? Up on the mountain? The burst of light and it's burning up there."

"It can't be burning on the mountain, Clara. The rain is torrential."

"It may not be raining that hard up there. And I know what a fire on the mountain looks like. Anyway, it's been a dry summer and fall. The whole mountain could go up in flames. It was such a loud burst of light . . . and such noise. Didn't you hear the explosion? It could be a plane crash, Stan. You know planes have crashed on that mountain before."

"Lightning and thunder. That's all it is. Come back to bed."

"It's too late for more, Stan. I have to get home. Don will be coming home. I have to fix his supper. It's dark as night out there, Stan. And the mountain is burning up there. I can still see the light . . . the flames."

Stan rose from the bed and padded over to the window. "Where? I don't see it." He had come under false pretenses, though. He wasn't looking at the mountain. He just wanted to come up behind her, to envelop her in his arms again, to take her again.

But she moved away from him and over to the chair where she'd folded and placed her clothes. "I have to go. Someone needs to telephone the fire department and tell them about that fire. It could race down here to Crozet . . . if the rain doesn't douse it. The summer and fall have been so dry."

"I'll call. After you're gone," Stan said, taking his pleasure at seeing her dress herself.

But of course he didn't call.

The flash of light up on the Blue Ridge had caught Don's attention as he'd been pulling the plants outside the covered entrance of the Blue Ridge Builders store on Route 250 between Charlottesville and Crozet closer in to the wall from the pelting rain. And was there still a glow up there? A fire? Bad time of year for there to be a fire on the mountain. It could burn thousands of acres as dry as the season had been. But it was raining cats and dogs. Surely that would put any fire out.

Maybe he should call Clara, though, and ask her if she'd seen anything from Crozet. He went back into the store and to the manager's booth and rang home. There was no answer, though. Strange. It wasn't long before he'd be off. She'd normally be fixing dinner now.

A half hour later, he looked up at the mountain on his way out of the store. It still looked like there was a fire going up there, despite the rain. He couldn't tell if it was spreading, but he didn't want to assume that it wasn't. He fished his cell phone out of his pocket and punched in 911. Someone needed to report it.

Clara was in the kitchen when he entered the house. Her hair was wet, slicked down the sides of her head.

"I called earlier and no one answered," he said as he came up behind and encircled her waist with his arms.

"I must have been in the shower," she said. "Dinner will be a little late. I went to the mailbox and got soaked, so I took time to shower when I came in."

"I think there's a fire on the mountain. Maybe from the lightning with the storm. Did you see the flash or hear anything?"

"No. Guess I was in the shower then too. Haven't been out of the house other than going to the mailbox. I hope someone reported it. Even though it's raining, it's a bad time for there to be a fire on the mountain."

"Yes, I called it in."

"Good. Why don't you take a beer into the den and relax. Dinner's going to be a little late."

* * * *

"Did you see that, Hank?"

"What?"

"I thought I saw a blip on the screen . . . a low-flying plane. But when I looked, it blanked out."

"There aren't any planes up there in this soup, Brian."

The two air controllers at Charlottesville's CHO airport were taking a break. They hadn't left the tower—there were regulations against that—but they had stood up from their consoles and were standing watching the rain pelt the tarmac, drinking coffee, and discussing UVa's football chances again Brigham Young on Saturday. There weren't any planes reported in their airspace and there shouldn't be for a while. The thunderstorm was too strong. All of the scheduled landings at CHO had been shunted up to Maryland for the time being.

"Yeah, I guess you're right," Brian said. "We supposed to be getting a storm like this on Saturday's game day, do you think?"

* * * *

Travis was jolted out of his recliner by the explosion and flash of light.

"Shit, that was a close one," he muttered. He was alone in his cabin near the top of the Blue Ridge overlooking Crozet, but he lived alone and often talked to himself. He'd downed enough beers tonight—being skittish about being in a log cabin on the mountain during a heavy thunderstorm like this.

"This ain't doin' the crop any good," he exclaimed. He went over to a window looking down toward the valley. It was bright as day out there.

"Damn," he growled. The mountain was on fire. And right down there where he had his field of weed. It was raining buckets and still the mountain was burning. Must have been some lightning strike. Of course it was to be expected as little rain as they'd had for weeks. And now it was raining buckets and still the mountain was burning. And maybe his weed was burning.

He reached for his cell phone but then put it back down on the table. What if his weed field really was burning and the firefighters could smell it in the air? Wouldn't take much to tag him with that. His was the only cabin up here anywhere close to the field, and he had a history of being caught growing weed.

Instead of making a call, he went around the cabin turning off lights and such and tracking down his boots and rain parka. Let someone else get involved in reporting this shit. He wasn't anywhere near here. Hadn't been here for months. Was stayin' with his cousin down on the western side of the mountain in Verona.

Travis had to think. Was Shane out of jail yet? He must of been. And if he wasn't, there was Travis' ma up in Front Royal. She'd put him up and swear he'd been living with her all year if it came to that.

He lowered his head and ran through the rain to his Ford 150 truck and drove the winding track up to the Skyline Drive and then down the western slope of Afton Mountain. He hoped his cabin didn't go up in the fire, but if it did maybe that would help cover his little enterprise. Well, not so little.

Shit, he thought. And it was just about ready to harvest. Well, maybe the rain would put the fire out before anyone came looking and he'd be back in the cabin by the end of the week.

* * * *

The fire brigade from Crozet met the firefighter unit from the Shenandoah National Park Service at a lookout parking area on the Skyline Drive above where their spotters had located the fire on the eastern slope of the mountains. As the brigade captain's fire truck was pulling into the parking area, it almost ran into a red Ford 150 truck careening along the parkway toward the Afton Mountain entrance.

The rain was beginning to let up—which was both good and bad news. It would make it easier for them to work their way down the mountainside to the fire scene. But if the fire was still going, it could easily flare up and out of control without the rain working against it.

The foliage was so dense that it took the firefighting crews a couple of hours to work their way down the mountainside. By then the rain had stopped altogether. There were still rivulets of fire around a charred clearing when they got there and some of the men were directed to chase after those with their extinguishers.

Most of the men, however, gathered around the cause of the fire. What had once been a Beechcraft Baron aircraft had crashed into the mountain. The wreckage was black and still smoking when the men approached.

Inside the craft they found two bodies. They were burned beyond recognition other than being able to be identified as a male and female. The senior park service ranger called the airport at Charlottesville, only to be informed that there were no aircraft within two hundred miles that were unaccounted for and, in fact, no known light aircraft flights in the vicinity since the strong thunderstorm had closed the airport and the adjacent airspace.

Days later there still had been no report of a missing flight and a crash landing of Boeing 707 passenger airliner at Richmond airport three days after the burned out Beechcraft had been found knocked the mystery flight downing on Afton Mountain out of the news.

~

Final Flight will soon be available in e-book and paperback at all online book retailers.

Introduction to the *Final Flight* Short Story Collection

Both the Shenandoah National Park Service and the fire stations on the Virginia Piedmont plain on the eastern side of the Blue Ridge Mountains are called during a nighttime thunderstorm. A small forest fire, reportedly preceded by an explosion, has been observed on the eastern slope of Afton Mountain. The rain is heavy and the site of the fire is remote. By the time the park rangers have descended to the site and the firefighters have ascended to it, the fire has essentially been doused by the rain. What the crews find is the smoldering fuselage of a twin-engine Beechcraft Baron aircraft. In the smoldering ruins are two bodies, determined to be that of a man and a woman, burned beyond ready identification.

No one reports missing a plane—or a man or woman—for that matter, and no flight plan was on file for a Beechcraft Baron in the Central Virginia airspace for that night. What could be the story behind this crash, which is taken from the scenario, albeit not the time frame, of an actual occurrence in 1963?

From this scenario, Olivia Stowe has woven eight separate short stories on events that fit the facts and that could plausibly explain what brought that plane and those two people to oblivion in the Blue Ridge Mountains. Preceding these stories is an additional story, "Fire on the Mountain," giving accounts of the crash from the various perspectives of those on the ground that night.

~

About the Author

Olivia Stowe is a published author under different names and in other dimensions of fiction and nonfiction and lives quietly in a university town with an indulgent spouse.

Our authors like to receive feedback and appreciate reviews being posted at Goodreads and other sites.

All Olivia's books, except the "Bundles," are available in paperback and e-book.

Mystery Romance
Restoring the Castle

The Charlotte Diamond Mystery Series
By The Howling (Book 1)
Retired with Prejudice (Book 2)
Coast to Coast (Book 3)
An Inconvenient Death (Book 4)
What's The Point? (Book 5)
White Orchid Found (Book 6)
Curtain Call (Book 7)
Horrid Honeymoon (Book 8)
Follow the Palm (Book 9)
Making Room at Christmas (Seasonal Special)
Cassandra's last Spotlight (Seasonal Special)

Charlotte Diamond Mysteries Bundle 1 (Books 1&2)
Charlotte Diamond Mysteries Bundle 2 (Books 3&4)
Charlotte Diamond Mysteries Bundle 3 (Books 5&6)

The Savannah Series
Chatham Square
Savannah Time

Olivia's Inspirational Christmas collections
Christmas Seconds (2011)
Spirit of Christmas (2010)